34

SAVING MAGNOLIA

BROTHERHOOD PROTECTORS WORLD

JEN TALTY

Twisted Page Press LLC

SAVING MAGNOLIA
A Brotherhood Protectors Novella
Book 2 in the Saving Series

USA Today Bestselling Author
JEN TALTY

BROTHERHOOD PROTECTORS

ORIGINAL SERIES BY ELLE JAMES

Brotherhood Protectors Series

Montana SEAL (#1)

Bride Protector SEAL (#2)

Montana D-Force (#3)

Cowboy D-Force (#4)

Montana Ranger (#5)

Montana Dog Soldier (#6)

Montana SEAL Daddy (#7)

Montana Ranger's Wedding Vow (#8)

Montana SEAL Undercover Daddy (#9)

Cape Cod SEAL Rescue (#10)

Montana SEAL Friendly Fire (#11)

Montana SEAL's Mail-Order Bride (#12)

SEAL Justice (#13)

Ranger Creed (#14)

Delta Force Rescue (#15)

Montana Rescue (Sleeper SEAL)

Hot SEAL Salty Dog (SEALs in Paradise)

Hot SEAL Hawaiian Nights (SEALs in Paradise)

NOTE FROM JEN TALTY

Welcome to my brand-new *Saving Series* in the BROTHERHOOD PROTECTORS world. I hope you will enjoy this as much as you did the *Out of the Wild series.* Not only do continue to use the characters that Elle James has created in her BROTHERHOOD PROTECTOR series, but many of my characters from the *Out of the Wild series* show up. I want to thank Elle James for this wonderful opportunity!

"Deadly Secrets is the best of romance and suspense in one hot read!" *NYT Bestselling Author Jennifer Probst*

"A charming setting and a steamy couple heat up the pages in a suspenseful story I couldn't put down!" *NY Times and USA today Bestselling Author Donna Grant*

"Jen Talty's books will grab your attention and pull you into a world of relatable characters, strong personalities, humor, and believable storylines. You'll laugh, you'll cry, and you'll rush to get the next book she releases!"

Natalie Ann USA Today Bestselling Author

"I positively loved *In Two Weeks*, and highly recommend it. The writing is wonderful, the story is fantastic, and the characters will keep you coming back for more. I can't wait to get my hands on future installments of the NYS Troopers series."
Long and Short Reviews

"*In Two Weeks* hooks the reader from page one. This is a fast paced story where the development of the romance grabs you emotionally and the suspense keeps you sitting on the edge of your chair. Great characters, great writing, and a believable plot that can be a warning to all of us." *Desiree Holt, USA Today Bestseller*

"*Dark Water* delivers an engaging portrait of wounded hearts as the memorable characters take you on a healing journey of love. A mysterious death brings danger and intrigue into the drama, while sultry passions brew into a believable plot that melts the reader's heart. Jen Talty pens an entertaining romance that grips the heart as the colorful and dangerous story unfolds into a chilling ending." *Night Owl Reviews*

"This is not the typical love story, nor is it the typical mystery. The characters are well rounded and interesting." *You Gotta Read Reviews*

"*Murder in Paradise Bay* is a fast-paced romantic thriller with plenty of twists and turns to keep you guessing until the end. You won't want to miss this one..." *USA Today bestselling author Janice Maynard*

To Harper, Hayden, and Sabre.

CHAPTER 1

MAGNOLIA CLARKE COULD TELL a lot about a person by the tattoo they picked or had her design.

The rose made out of hundred-dollar bills with the initials *FC* off to the side told her more about the man sitting in her chair than she ever wanted to know about another soul.

Ever.

She did her best to keep her hand steady as she adjusted the light over his shoulder and wiped his back before going back to her design. The tattoo was relatively intricate, and she was already four hours into it, with another one to go.

She'd done the exact same design at least twenty times when she'd first become a tattoo artist, and each time she wanted to vomit. But back then, she'd been under the control of her crazy-ass parents. On her twentieth birthday, she packed up her things and left Charleston, South Carolina. She lived in fear for four years until she'd seen the news about her father's death and her mother's demise.

Until a week ago, she'd been breathing easy for the last three years.

When Calvin Dugget sent her the image and called to make his appointment, she had tried to push him off, explaining how booked she was, that it would be weeks before she could fit him in.

He was fine with that and only asked to be put on a waiting list. Unfortunately, her one and only employee happened to find him an earlier appointment.

She could still refuse and tell him to tell her mother to fuck off.

Mommy dearest would not only be pissed.

But she'd take revenge.

Of course, Magnolia could be paranoid. Her mother was in prison. Her father was dead. And their counterfeit and money laundering business completely defunct, along with whatever other criminal activities they had been involved in, and the list was long.

But if her mother had managed to somehow create a new crew from behind bars, she'd eventually have all her team brand themselves with her chosen ink.

And of course, her initials had to be part of that design.

Magnolia swallowed. There were a lot of rose-shaped money tattoos out there, but this was too close to what she used to do for her mother, including a small magnolia that her mother made her put on every tattoo right by the initials *FC*.

Magnolia adjusted the light. "How are you holding up?"

"I'm good," Calvin said. "This ain't my first rodeo."

"I didn't ask, but are you from around here?" She'd lived in the foothills of the Crazy Mountains in Montana for three years and other than her clients, which were mostly a bunch of ex-military dudes that ran a protection detail business, a bunch of local ranchers, cowboys, and a few rich socialites who either wanted a tasteful, but hidden tatt, or wanted to get back at daddy, she hadn't made any real personal connections. Magnolia normally might keep to herself, but she knew a lot of the townspeople, and this man wasn't anyone she'd seen before.

Not even at Hiccups, a local watering hole that brought in people from counties fifty miles away, especially when Aces was playing. They were quite the country band.

"I'm just here for a couple of weeks. Visiting an old friend."

"That's nice. Is he who recommended me to you?" She pressed her pen into his skin, starting on the faded image of a magnolia while trying not to cry. It was stupid, really. That part of her life was nothing

3

but a blip on her radar. If she blinked at the right moment, she wouldn't even know it existed. But staring at Calvin's muscular back with a money rose tattoo, all the pain and suffering her family created for many innocent people smacked her right between the eyes.

"You've come highly recommended by just about everyone who has a tattoo in the area. I'm starting to really like it here."

"Yeah. Why's that?"

"Where I'm from, in the summer it gets real humid and gross. Not to mention we have hurricanes. Those are never fun."

She continued with what used to be her mother's signature design, and her namesake. She resented the hell out of the damn flower and had thought about changing her name for years, but there was a small part of her that wanted to hold on to where she'd come from.

Just to remind herself what she'd managed to escape.

"Would it be okay with you if I took a picture for the wall?" She bit down on her lower lip. The tattoo artist who'd taken over after Magnolia had taken off did a shit job comparatively. Her mother used to send her emails with the hatchet job, begging Magnolia to return or at the very least, let her mother know where she was so she could send her crew to her for the tattoos.

"I'd rather you didn't," he said.

Her mother demanded perfection and prided herself on having the best employees.

Magnolia gagged on the thought.

"I hope you will change your mind. I keep a copy of all my designs anyway."

"Are you done?"

"Just about." She swiped at his red, raw skin and admired her work. She really was good at her job. Now she needed to be excellent at saving her ass. She pushed her rolling chair across the room where she picked up a mirror and opened the drawer where she stashed her small handgun. Being able to shoot a glass bottle at fifty feet away was the only lesson she'd been grateful that she'd taken from her past. Glancing over her shoulder, she stuffed her weapon in her oversized front pocket. "Would you like to see?"

"Damn straight." Calvin sat up. He had broad shoulders and a hulk-type body. Not to mention he had to be at least six foot four. She shivered. If she were one hundred and twenty pounds soaking wet, that would be a miracle. And she didn't stand taller than five five on a good day.

He could squash her like a bug before she had a chance to pull out her gun.

She rolled the tall mirror over to him and handed him the smaller one.

"Wow. I love it."

"That's great. I'm glad."

Calvin handed him her phone. "Can you take a picture of it? I need to send it to my girlfriend."

"Sure." She inhaled sharply, focusing on her artwork and not her racing heart. "Here you go." She let out a puff of air. "Here's some lotion. I know you know the drill."

"I do. Thanks." He took his shirt and pulled it over his head.

She couldn't help but feel as though danger lurked in a dark corner waiting to attack as they made their way to the front of the store.

He handed her an envelope with a wad of cash. "You'll find a nice little tip in there for you." He leaned over the counter and smiled. His dark eyes turned ominous under the florescent lights. "Next time someone comes to you with this design, don't try to push them out or deny them altogether."

Her breath caught in her throat. Slowly, she slipped her hand into her pocket.

He shook his head, making a clucking noise. "I wouldn't do that if I were you. My gun is bigger, more powerful, but I won't shoot to kill, and neither will the two men outside. Nope. They will enjoy you first, and then they will toss you at the mercy of your mother."

"You have me mistaken for someone else," she said behind a tight jaw. She had been damned no matter how she'd played her cards. If she'd continued to tell him no, he probably would have kidnapped her or killed her.

And since she'd inked him for her mother, they believed they had some control over her, and they did, to a certain extent.

Calvin laughed. "No, Magnolia. I know exactly who you are, and your mother and I are excited to have you on the team."

She shook her head. Her vision blurred. Her chest tightened. This couldn't be happening. No fucking way was she going back to inking her mother's crew.

No.

Fucking.

Way.

She would die first.

She pressed her hands flat on the counter. "You tell my mother she can go fuck herself."

"Not the right answer."

"How the hell is she managing all this from behind bars?"

"Oh. You haven't heard, have you?"

No. No. No. Please don't say her mother was getting out of prison.

"Heard what?"

"New evidence has been entered into the court regarding your father's death, proving your mother didn't murder him, and she's going to be released in a few months since she's paid her debt to society for her other crimes."

Suddenly it became difficult to fill her lungs. Magnolia had suspected her mother hadn't murdered her father. Well, not with her own two hands.

Her mother didn't have the stomach to kill, but she had no problem hiring someone to do it. So when Joey, 'the bat' Bronco, a man her mother used often, was arrested for her fathers premature departure from life, Magnolia knew without a doubt, her mother was guilty as the sky was blue.

"They already picked up Joey and he confessed. Unfortunately, He had a lot of enemies and he didn't last more than ten days in jail. He took a shiv in the heart while exercising in the yard."

Magnolia hadn't heard that name in years. Letting him get away with murder was a small price to pay in order to make sure her mother never saw the light of day. "What exactly did he confess to? And did he say who hired him if it wasn't my mother?" When the story broke, curiosity had gotten the better of Magnolia and she found herself reaching out to an old friend who told her that it had been rumored that her mother's boyfriend, some dude by the name of Big Cal, took out the hit on her father, but it had never been proven. Since the weapon had been Flower's and her prints had been all over the gun, there was enough evidence to convince a jury.

"Some guy that was sleeping with your mother." He winked.

"Was that guy named Big Cal?"

"Could have been," he said.

She shivered. "You're Big Cal."

"I'm impressed," he said with a beaming smile. He had some seriously white teeth. So bright she found herself squinting as she stared at them.

"Why are you just now getting my mom's tattoo?"

"Timing. It's all about timing," he said. "So, if you know what's good for you, which I'm sure you do, you'll take good care of our friends as we send them to you. That's all we want. Nothing more. Nothing less. Do that, and we'll all get along just fine."

"It's a long way from Charleston, South Carolina, just to get a fucking tattoo."

Calvin lifted his baseball cap off the coatrack and sauntered toward the main door. He gripped the handle with his massive hand. "When your mother gets her walking papers, we're relocating."

As soon as he was outside, she raced across the room and locked the door. Leaning against the wood, she slid to the floor and clutched her chest. Her mother wouldn't be satisfied with Magnolia simply inking her crew. No. Her mother wanted more.

But what?

Pop, pop, pop, pop, pop!

She dropped to her stomach and crawled across the uneven wood planks, hiding behind the counter while the roar of gunfire echoed all around her.

Her mother didn't want more.

Her mother wanted her dead.

She found her phone and dialed 9-1-1. A few more shots pelted the building before the store went eerily quiet. The smell of bitter smoke filled the air. Her mother would require proof of death. She pulled out her weapon, inched to the right, and aimed for the front of the store.

Well, if Big Cal walked back through those doors, the only proof mommy dearest would get was that her boyfriend was a dumbfuck. He should have killed her while he was standing in the shop instead of trying to make it look like some random whatever.

The sound of an engine revving made the hair on the back of her neck stand up on end.

"9-1-1. What's your emergency?"

"This is Magnolia Clarke. I'm at Mags Tattoo Parlor just outside of town. Shots were fired at my—"

"Yes. Someone called that in already. Where are you?"

"Inside. But it seems to have stopped."

"Stay right where you are. Help is less than five minutes away."

The door rattled.

She squeezed the trigger. She'd never killed anyone, and she didn't know if she could, but she didn't want to die today. Not at the hands of anyone connected to the bitch that birthed her. She blinked. Perspiration beaded across her forehead.

A boot stepped onto the floor.

Holding her breath, she kept her gaze glued to a

bronzed belt buckle as a tall familiar man entered the lobby with a weapon drawn. "Whoa, Magnolia. Put that thing down. It's me. Dewey."

She dropped the gun and let out a gasp, cupping her cheeks, hoping she didn't start bawling like a baby, especially in front of Dewey Stone.

He knelt by her side, tipping her chin up with his thumb and forefinger. He'd pushed his shades on top of his head, which had taken some of his thick, sandy-brown hair with them. He had this scruffy, sexy hair style that looked like he hadn't bothered even running a comb through it, only she suspected he spent hours on it. He had piecing blue eyes that captured her attention. She couldn't turn away if she tried.

"Are you okay?" He patted down her arms, adjusting her smock, smoothing his hands over her jeans, down her thighs, even across her calves. "Did you get hit?"

She shook her head. "I don't think so. I heard a car." She wasn't sure what she should say to Dewey, if anything at all. She needed to empty her bank accounts, sell what she could, and leave by the end of the week.

Fuck.

She needed to sneak out in the middle of the night, when no one was looking, especially Big Cal.

"Maddog and I saw some guy jump in a sedan and

race out of here like a bat out of hell. Any idea who was shooting at you and why?"

"No," she said quickly.

"Seriously?" He arched a brow as he helped her to a standing position. Sirens echoed in the background. "Maddog and I had dinner with a client in town. We saw the same vehicle in the parking lot two hours ago. Whoever shot up your place, you'd been giving them a tattoo. So, what happened?"

Out of the corner of her eye, she saw a police car skid to a stop not far from the main entrance. If she told the cops, they would call the authorities in South Carolina, who would question her mother, and it would just make things worse.

"I can't. Not in front of the police."

"You mean to tell me you're going to lie to law enforcement about what went down here?" Dewey said as he rubbed his thumb across her cheek.

"You don't understand. I have to. I need you to go along with me. Please. I'm begging."

He let out a long breath and pursed his lips. "All right, but after they take your statement, you're coming back to my place and telling me what the fuck is going on, got it? Otherwise, I'm hauling your pretty little ass down to the station myself."

"Okay." She'd have to find a way to ditch Dewey, which was too bad. She'd had the hots for him for a while now, but he never gave her a second glance, though he'd certainly become addicted to getting tattoos lately. His latest one was some kind of a massive fighter jet across his back with a helmet and his name written across it. It had taken her weeks to get the design right, and now she figured it would take at least five sessions to finish it.

Only now, someone else would have to do it for Dewey.

She was going to miss living in the foothills of the Crazy Mountains. Montana had been the first place that ever felt like home.

DEWEY CLOSED out the one browser and pulled up his security system on his laptop. He didn't trust that Magnolia wouldn't try to climb out his bathroom window and take off in the middle of the night. He leaned back in his chair, sipping his beer. "The car was returned to the airport, and Calvin Dugget boarded a plane headed to Atlanta, but I don't think that is his final destination."

"What else do we know about this guy?" Maddog asked. "And why doesn't Magnolia want the locals involved?"

That had been an interesting tale that Magnolia had spun, and he doubted she'd lied about any of it. No one made that kind of shit up, but he suspected she left a lot of details out and that was information he planned on obtaining soon enough, especially considering what Dewey had just found out. "He owns five restaurants in Charleston, South Carolina. He's on the FBI's hot list for money laundering, counterfeiting, and being an all-around dick, but he's got a few buddies in the local police department that seem to be in his pocket."

"So, now give me what you're not telling me." Maddog stood and leaned against the wall by the front window of Dewey's house. When Dewey had left the Navy at the ripe old age of thirty-eight and came to Montana, he decided it was time to put down roots. He bought an old farmhouse, and he'd been fixing it up for the last two years.

Now that his home was complete, all he needed was to find himself the love of a good woman. Every time he considered dating a lady, he'd walk into Mags Tattoo Parlor and stare into her sandy-colored eyes and wish he wasn't so hung up on two facts.

Her age.

And the darkness that lurked behind her sweet smile. He'd lived a crazy life; he didn't want baggage in his future.

Well, now he knew why she kept the world at arm's length.

The sound of water shutting off in the master bedroom caught his attention. Magnolia was a free spirit, which is what attracted him to her in the first place. It's why he kept coming up with new tattoos to get so he could spend more time with her. It wasn't like he was all that into scarring his body. When he'd entered the Naval Academy, inking his body was a rite of passage. When he became a fighter pilot, he felt the need to have his squad forever etched in his skin.

He did the same when he joined the Brotherhood Protectors, and ever since then, he'd become slightly addicted to tattoos.

Or maybe it was Magnolia.

Didn't matter. He had a good five sessions left to finish the one that would take up half his back. He'd been hoping during that time he'd be able to get past the idea she was only twenty-seven.

His buddy Clayton, whose wife was fifteen years younger, kept reminding him that age was just a number and Magnolia was a grown-ass woman. Thirteen years wasn't the end of the world, not at this stage in the game.

Until tonight, he'd told himself since she wasn't even thirty yet; she'd barely seen the world. That she hadn't had enough time to know what she wanted out life or where she wanted to take it.

Only both her parents were hardened criminals. She had to have seen things that would make the average person's hair curl. That he could relate to, though from a different perspective. His childhood had been all rainbows and unicorns. It had been easy to bury his head in the sand. That might have been why he'd sought out the all-elusive adrenaline rush. It was as if he had to pinch himself extra hard to make sure he was alive.

Until he almost died.

"Magnolia lied to the police. Calvin had been a customer. She'd just finished up with him before he decided to shoot up her store."

Maddog turned. "You've got to be fucking kidding me. Why would she do that? More importantly, why would you let her?"

That was the million-dollar question, and he wasn't entirely sure he had a good answer. "Partly because her mother is Flower Clarke."

"That means nothing to me."

Up until a half hour ago, it meant absolutely nothing to Dewey either. He was pretty clueless and had a lot of reading and research to do on the subject of Flower Clarke, her late husband Glenn Clarke, and Big Cal Dugget, Flower's current boyfriend and biggest supporter.

Not to mention he was the same man who had tried to kill Magnolia, a point that Dewey took personally.

"Flower is currently in prison, though she's up to be released in a couple of months after serving consecutive terms for money laundering and counterfeiting. She was supposed to be locked away for life for murdering her husband, but that was overturned because of new evidence."

"And all of this was left out when she interviewed with the locals?" Maddog asked.

"Yup."

"Did you know this before or after and did Magnolia tell you or did you find this out on your own?"

"She told me about who she was and that her mom sent that asshole over to make a point. She doesn't think Big Cal was supposed to kill her but send a message. I would have to agree based on the bullet holes."

"They were all pretty high. Not a single hole lower than six feet."

"Yeah. If you want to murder someone that way, you tend to aim lower."

"What does Hank know?" Maddog asked.

"I haven't filled him in yet," Dewey said, but Hank had to have some idea of what had been going on with Magnolia because he'd been keeping a file on her, and Hank didn't do that unless he suspected something. But for now, Dewey wasn't about to toss anyone under the bus. Magnolia had her reasons for flying under the radar. "I want to keep her story with the locals as tight to the cuff as possible. At least for now."

"You've got to tell Hank."

He nodded. Fuck. He shifted his laptop and stared at the camera angled outside the window from his first-floor master bedroom facing the woods. "We've got a runner."

"Where the fuck does she think she's going to go?"

"I don't know, but she's not going to get far." Dewey stood.

"You want me to see if I can get someone to stay here tonight? Help you keep an eye on her?"

"No. We'll be fine. I'll touch base in the morning. If you happen to talk to Hank before I do, let him know I plan on reaching out before lunch."

"You got it." Maddog pulled open the side door and jogged toward his vehicle.

Dewey checked the app on his phone, getting a lock on Magnolia's exact location. He took off in a full-out sprint, circling around ahead of her so he could cut her off at the pass. Of course, he had to be careful considering she was resourceful, and he suspected she would have figured out a way to take her handgun. Just to be safe, he rested his hand on the butt of his weapon as he leaned against a tree. He eyed her scurrying through the woods, constantly glancing over her shoulder while staring at her cell, which illuminated her angelic face, showing off her near platinum blond hair.

He was going to scare her one way or the other. He cleared his throat. "Where do you think you're going?"

She jumped. Gasped. And dropped her cell. "Mother trucker."

"Sorry." He doubled-timed it and bent over, snatching up her phone. "What the fuck are you doing, Magnolia?"

"What does it look like?"

She raised her palms to the sky, then smacked them to her thighs. "And why do you care?"

"Well, for starters, I have an appointment in two days to work on my tattoo on my back. I can't go around with it only partially done."

"I'll give the design to someone else."

'You're seriously planning on up and leaving town, just like that?" He snapped his fingers.

"You don't understand. Big Cal? He might be gone for now, but he's coming back. And he's bringing with him a boatload of trouble. I need to be on a different planet when that happens."

"No. You need to be right here where I can protect you." He curled his fingers around her thin, but firm forearm.

She shrugged free. "You can't protect me from my mother. No one can."

"That's bullshit. Now let's go back to my place. I've got a killer apple pie in the fridge and some ice cream in the freezer. We can crack open a nice bottle of red—"

"Are you fucking kidding me?" She dug her heels into the dirt path. "My mother sent Big Cal to warn me that if I don't do what she wants, the next time he ain't going to miss. So, the next time, I ain't gonna fucking be here. Get the picture?"

"Loud and clear," he said, holding up his hands as if she were holding a weapon to his chest. "But your plan is a recipe for disaster, if you even have one."

"I'm working on it."

"All right. Why don't you come inside and at least tell me what it is and maybe I can help." He'd sell his soul to the devil right now to get her to agree to stay even a few hours. Anything to hear her plan so he could rip holes in it and prove to her she should let him and the rest of the Brotherhood protect her from whatever her mother had in store.

She laughed. "You don't want to help me."

"I know you're scared." He let out a long breath. "I know you think running and starting over somewhere else is the answer. But they will hunt you down. At least if you stay here, you have an army of ex-military men and women at your fingertips."

"I can't afford you."

"Finish my tattoo for free and we'll call it even."

"I don't have any of my equipment." She stuffed her hands in her pockets, kicked the ground, and started inching her way back toward his house.

"We'll pick it up tomorrow."

"I'm not agreeing to any of this other than crashing here one night," she said, glancing in his direction. "Staying here will not only be the death of me, but she'll kill anyone who gets in her way, and I won't be responsible for that."

He pressed his hand on the small of her back and chuckled. "I spent an entire career as a fighter pilot trying to get myself killed. I failed. Do you seriously think I'm going to let your mother or her asshole boyfriend or anyone else for that matter do me in?" Resting his hand on her hip, he held her body close. She smelled like a combination of his musky soap and a crisp sour apple. He resisted the urge to lean in and take a huge whiff of her slightly damp hair.

For over a year, Magnolia had been entering his thoughts and dreams, tormenting his mind and soul with images of a life he never thought he wanted until he'd set foot in Montana.

But Dewey hadn't ever been very smooth with the ladies. Sure, he'd had his share of short-term love affairs, but he'd always been the kind of man that preferred the roar of an engine to the arms and legs of a woman wrapped around his body. In his youth, he spent his days racing cars, bikes, and boats. Once he took to the skies, that was it. He'd found home. Coming face-to-face with the enemy, dodging bullets at Mach five, that was better than any sex he'd ever had.

Only fantasizing about Magnolia left him wondering what he might have been missing out on all these years.

He led her to the back patio off the master

bedroom. He tugged off the covers from a couple of lounge chairs. "Make yourself comfortable. I'll go get the wine and pie."

"Thanks. I'm actually starving."

"I'll be right back." He waggled his finger under her nose. "Don't go rushing off. I don't really feel like chasing you down again." Quickly, he raced into the house, gathering everything he needed, including his laptop. He wanted to continue to monitor his cameras and the rest of the security on his property. He also wanted her to see what he had in place.

Not so she would know there was no chance of her disappearing, but so she'd feel safe with him in his home.

He set a tray down on the coffee table before pouring two glasses of red wine.

"What's that plastic thing?"

"It's an aerator. I'm too lazy to decanter and let it breathe, so this opens it up."

She took the beverage, lifting it to her nose, then closed her eyes and inhaled. She blinked. Her plump lips curled over the rim, and the dark liquid eased into her mouth. She moaned. "Wow. Not only does that little gadget work, but this is some seriously good-ass wine. It must be expensive."

"Not really. Only about thirty dollars a bottle."

"Whatever it is, it's really good." She held up her glass. "So, you were one of those death wish kind of military guys. You were a Navy Pilot, right?"

He nodded. "I flew a Super Hornet, which is what is going on my back."

"Isn't that what the Blue Angles fly?"

"That would be correct," he said. "It's an awesome aircraft, and I'm even more impressed you know that."

"When I was a little girl, my father took me to see them once. It was mesmerizing." She tucked a piece of her blond hair behind her ears. It had a slight wave to it, though she normally wore it pin straight. "I can't imagine being in a machine that powerful."

"It's pretty amazing," he said. "While those days are long behind me, I still like to fly."

"I've seen you and your little plane." She shifted to her side and smiled. "I like to ride my bike down by the airfield and watch the small planes. I've always dreamed of taking flying lessons."

"Well now. I just got my instructors license to give me something to do on the side when I don't have a protection detail. Why don't you let me teach you?"

She shook her head. "Wanting to do something and actually doing it are two entirely different things. Besides, I'm afraid of flying."

"Best way to get over that is to take over the controls." He reached out and batted her nose. He swallowed. What a dumb and insanely forward thing to do.

"I've never been on an airplane." She nibbled on

the pie. The ice cream melted the second it touched her lips.

Shit. He was not going to sleep a wink tonight.

"Not even a commercial one?" he asked.

"Nope. When I came here from South Carolina, I drove my beat-up old Jeep until it died somewhere in Texas. I stayed there for a couple of years working two jobs until I saved up enough money to buy my current ride. I lived a couple other places until I ended up here, but anywhere I went, it was always on the open road."

"Your Jeep is a hunk of shit, and you are in desperate need of some new tires before winter hits."

"I'm well aware." She swirled a piece of hair between her fingers.

He reached out and traced the simple heartbeat tattoo on the inside of her wrist. She wasn't covered in tattoos. At least not her exposed skin. But the ones she did have were small and simple.

And he suspected had meaning.

"Tell me about this one."

"It's actually my very first tattoo. I got it when I was fifteen."

"That's young," he said.

She laughed. "My parents were criminals. They didn't give a shit. But it's when I decided I wanted to be a tattoo artist." She turned her shoulder and lowered her shirt, showing off a butterfly with an eye in the center. "This was my second one. I was sixteen."

He tugged at the fabric so he could see the entire pattern. "Wow. That's beautiful."

"Thanks. I designed it myself. The guy that I did my apprenticeship with inked it. Actually, he inked most of my tatts."

"What's the meaning behind those two?"

"The heartbeat is to remind me not to let my mother and father break me."

"I like that," he said.

"And the butterfly with the eye is more about continuing to grow and change and keeping the focus on the future, not the past. Only it looks like the past just caught up with me."

"Sometimes that happens." He took her hand and traced the band of bracelet tattoos she had on her other wrist. One looked like a chain-link fence. Another had a number of charms that appeared to dangle from it, and a third was a series of words strung together to form a saying: *You are not the sum of where you came from; your soul is a combination of what you want to be and what you allow your heart to see and feel. Be strong. Be fierce. Be you.* "Where does this saying come from?"

"Kip Bowling, my mentor. He knew all about my mom and her insanity. He helped me get away from her to begin with."

"Where is he now?"

She took a long sip and swiped at her eyes. "Dead."

"Fuck. I'm sorry."

"That's what happens when you cross my mother."

He did a quick scan of his computer screen. Nothing jumped out at him. He lifted his cell and checked his text messages and emails, just in case.

Nothing.

"Since you've officially hired the Brotherhood Protectors—"

"I have not." She poked his chest. "The cost of your tattoo isn't even close, so don't go there. And I doubt that Patterson guy would allow it."

"You'd be surprised." He leaned closer. "What does your mother want from you? And don't lie to me. I can't help you if you start leaving things out or making shit up."

"It's honestly the dumbest thing in the world." She held up her phone. "She wants to send her new crew to me so I can put her gang tattoo on their bodies."

He took her cell and stared at the image. He'd never seen anything like it before. "You designed this, didn't you?"

"Unfortunately. It started out as a doodle when I was like ten. It snowballed into something else, and when I was sixteen and started working with Kip, my mom had me make some adjustments; we added the magnolia and my mom's initials, and that became her crew marking."

"Why you? Can't any tattoo artist copy it?"

"A lot won't. At least not exactly like that out of respect for the original artist, so that's one reason. But really, mommy dearest just wants to control me. She wants me to be part of the so-called family business. To maybe one day take it over and now that she's getting out of jail, she's going to push harder."

"Do you know when that's happening?"

"No. There is some hearing about all that in a week. She could be out shortly after that, or it could be months. My guess would be sooner rather than later. My mom is a master manipulator, which is why I need to be the fuck out of here ASAP, and this time I need to do it right."

"And what does that mean?"

"I need to change my name. Do you know anyone who can help me with that?"

He knew a few people who could make her disappear, and if it came down to that, he'd gladly make sure it happened. He took her chin between his thumb and forefinger. "I've got people on the ground in South Carolina when Big Cal lands. Let's work out a plan to keep you safe while we figure out how to make sure your mother either stays behind bars, or her freedom is short-lived."

Magnolia opened her mouth, but he hushed her with a short but powerful kiss. It wasn't passionate, or wet and sloppy, but it packed the kind of punch that should tell her that not only did he mean what he said about taking care of her, but that he also cared about her in ways he'd never expressed before.

Or at least that was the intent of the kiss. He had no idea if he pulled it off or not.

She fisted a wad of his T-shirt in her hand. "What the hell was that?"

"I've been dying to do that for about a year," he admitted.

"Well, your timing sucks."

"Generally speaking, that's true when it comes to women," he said with a chuckle. "But I do know people who could make you disappear. I just don't want that to happen. I'd prefer to defeat the enemy and keep you right here where I can keep doing this." He lifted her from the seat, cradling her in his lap. Her hot tongue reached inside his mouth and scorched his insides like gas being tossed on a fire.

She gripped his shoulders, digging her fingernails into his skin with unbridled passion.

He'd meant to only show her what could be, not start something that couldn't be stopped.

She broke off the kiss and stood. "Seriously? You've known me for almost two years, and you wait until someone shoots at me before you go and make a move? Or is that some weird Brotherhood thing to snag a client?"

He tapped his chest. "I'm offended."

"What you are is incredibly late to the game." She bent over, showing off what little cleavage she had, which wasn't really any, and he liked that.

Her breasts would get lost in his palms, and that just made his thumbs and fingers itch to feel her nipples tighten under his touch.

"You might have had a chance a few months ago." She chugged the rest of her wine.

He hopped to his feet. "Are you saying you were attracted to me a while ago, but not anymore?"

She patted his shoulder. "There isn't a woman who has blood in her veins that doesn't go weak in the knees when you enter the room, but that's not the point." She leaned in and kissed his cheek. "Now that my mother is all up in my junk, I can't have the distraction while I figure out how to keep her from ruining my life. No offense."

"None taken." He pulled open the sliding glass doors. "Only, trust me when I say, I'm exactly the kind of distraction you're going to need when this is over." He waved his hand in front of him. "And I will make damn sure it ends in such a way that you will have the opportunity to stay in Montana and get to know more than the ink you put on my skin."

CHAPTER 2

Magnolia spent the night tossing and turning, only she wasn't sure if it was from the anxiety of her mother's little message in the form of Big Cal and bullets, or Dewey's unexpected kiss.

And oh, what a kiss.

If she'd been wearing socks, they'd be knocked off.

Dewey was one of those guys she daydreamed about but would never consider asking out. Not because he was older. His maturity and sense of self made him all that more appealing. But she was never lucky enough to find the caliber of men like Dewey. Not that she'd ever tried. She liked living alone. She liked not having to answer to anyone, especially after having grown up with controlling criminal parents.

She glided her fingers across the wood railing as she made her way down the stairs. Dewey's home sat on what she guessed to be about ten acres of land. The house itself was two stories with three bedrooms upstairs and the master on the first floor. He had a thing for leather and dark colors, but it suited his quiet masculine personality, as did his Harley that he rode in the summer months and his souped-up custom F-250 he liked to show off during the winter. Dewey had a flare for flashy, powerful machines that made his presence known and could tear up the roadways.

She could relate to that; only her escape came in the form of a pen and ink.

Slowly, she eased down the hallway, through the family room, admiring the man's taste in oversized chairs that invited a person to relax and enjoy a peaceful afternoon in front of the fireplace or reading a book. Even though the place felt undone since he didn't have many wall hangings or knick-knacks on the shelves, it had a strong sense of home. She could tell he wanted this as his sanctuary. It was all about him, and being inside these walls was as if he'd wrapped his strong arms around her and held her tight in a protective hug.

"Good morning," Dewey said from behind the island in center of the kitchen. He wore a pair of jeans, a white T-shirt, and he held out a large mug with steam floating from the top. "Would you like some coffee?"

"I'd love some, thanks."

"I've got an egg, sausage, spinach, cheese, pepper, and onion frittata in the oven if you're hungry. It should be done in about ten minutes."

"Aren't you little Mr. Sam Homemaker." She took a slow sip of the hazelnut-tasting coffee. The hot liquid burned the back of her throat as she swallowed.

She kept a safe distance from everyone she'd met, not making close friends. It made for a lonely existence, but deep down, she always worried her mother would reach out from behind her prison walls and wreak havoc on Magnolia's life, which is why she kept one go bag in the back seat of her vehicle and one under her bed. She could never be too prepared.

But she'd gotten too comfortable in Montana. This had only been meant to be a short stint. Just enough to save up more money and move on to maybe North Dakota. The plan had been to jump from one random state to the next until her brain allowed her to completely trust in what the government had done, and that was to lock up her mother and throw away the key.

"I like food, and not just basic stuff, so I had to learn to cook."

"I'll hold my judgment until my taste buds have a chance to inspect the product."

"Trust me. It's going to be the best breakfast you've experienced since you moved here."

"We shall see." She made her way toward the

sliding glass doors. The morning sun appeared behind the mountains. The blue sky stretched on forever without a cloud to be seen anywhere. A couple of birds flew from one tree to the next as a slight breeze kicked up, rustling the leaves. "It's so beautiful here."

"I used to hate the quiet."

"Why?"

"When I was in the Navy and deployed, it was the silent times that were the most dangerous. It always meant that something crazy was about to happen. So, when I first moved out here, I couldn't stand sitting in the dead of night, listening only to the noise of the wild. It terrified me." His biceps flexed as he pulled open the door. "But now, I really enjoy the peace and quiet." He pointed to the table. "Have a seat. I'll bring out your feast."

"A girl could get used to this kind of treatment."

He leaned in and kissed her cheek. "Oh, it comes at a price."

"Do I want to know?"

"Probably not," he said with a chuckle and disappeared.

She let out a long breath, making herself comfortable in one of the chairs facing the mountain range. Tugging her cell out of her back pocket, she glanced at her messages. She'd been able to reschedule all of her appointments for today, but she still wasn't sure what to do about her shop, which was also her apartment. The man who owned the place was nice enough to let her turn the upstairs into a loft.

He wasn't going to be too thrilled when she called him to inform him of the damage. Of course, she'd have to pay for the repairs.

She glanced over her shoulder. Staying here was stupid. She was going to have to make Dewey understand that her only chance at freedom was a new identity and a geographical change.

But this time she'd do it right. This time she'd disappear so there was no way in hell mommy dearest could ever find her again.

Dewey emerged carrying a tray piled with food. The mix of hot peppers and onions with cheddar cheese melting over fluffy eggs filled her senses, making her stomach growl. She'd thought about what it might be like to wake up next to Dewey once or twice. She figured half of the women in Montana had wicked sexual fantasies about him. Not only did he have tight, thick muscles, but he had kind eyes, a sweet smile, and he was a damned gentleman.

"And you're not married or have a girlfriend?"

"Neither." He set a plate down in front of her and refreshed her coffee before making himself comfortable. "I didn't have time for relationships when I was in the Navy, and since I've been with the Brotherhood Protectors, I haven't found anyone interesting enough."

She filled her fork with the egg concoction and

stuff it in her mouth. "Oh, God. That's seriously really good."

"I'm glad you like." He raised his mug.

She waved her utensil in the air. She found herself wanting to know more and more about Dewey and where he came from, what he liked, disliked. What kept him up at night and what calmed his restless soul. "So, what constitutes interesting in a woman?"

"Well, for starters, any lady I end up with has to be smart and like tattoos." He winked.

"That's not very intriguing. I think you can do better."

"I don't know about that." He leaned in, resting his elbows on the table. "You're a bit of an enigma."

"Not really. I just like to keep to myself and now you know why."

"That makes you all that more appealing and sexy."

The corners of her mouth tugged upward into a brief smile. "Because I'm the daughter of a pair of notorious criminals?"

He chuckled. "Does it make me a whack job if my answer is a big fat yes and no."

"No. But that's only because you're already a nutcase."

He plopped a piece of cantaloupe in his mouth. "I used to be a crazy motherfucker with a death wish."

"What happened?"

"I died."

She coughed, choking on a small piece of onion. "Excuse me? Are you being serious? Like literally died as in your heart stopped beating?"

He held up a couple of fingers. "For nearly two minutes."

"I take it that happened on some dangerous mission." She had an image in her head of him being blown out of the sky in some dog fight or maybe being shot behind enemy lines. She'd heard some insane stories by many of his buddies while they sat in her chair and she inked their bodies, and she knew most of the time they added a bit of humor or sugar-coated what happened to ease the horror. "And before you tell me, thank you for your service."

"You know, you've said that to me a good dozen times."

"It should be said every day."

"You're a sweet girl."

"You don't know me." She rolled her eyes. "Now, tell me about this death experience. I've honestly never met anyone who actually went to heaven and came back."

"Well, I wouldn't say I met my maker. I don't remember flatlining." He flipped his shades down over his eyes and stared off into the sunrise. "We came across some hostiles in the sky over the Mediterranean Sea. It started as a game of chicken. I've gotten into those more times than I can count and normally, nothing ever comes of them. The enemy has their fun and turns around and goes home we do the same thing. I thought that day would be the same. It was an amazing dog fight. I honestly had never had so much fun in my life. The adrenaline rush was about as intense as I'd ever experienced." His voice rose an octave, and he tapped his finger rapidly on the ceramic top as his knee rattled, shaking the table. "Me and my team maneuvered between the bogies, and they showed off what their machines could do. It was as if we were using our planes to trash talk each other until they fired at us. It sounds strange, but it was totally unexpected."

"That does seem odd, since they engaged you in antagonistic battle. And isn't that what happens when you come across the enemy?"

"Granted, that wasn't the first time I've been shot at, but it's certainly not an everyday occurrence. As a matter of fact, it doesn't happen as often as you'd think. My missions are often fly in, do some damage, and fly out. Anyway, in the chaos, I lost both engines, ended up in a flat spin, and we had to eject. I don't remember anything that happened after my parachute opened. According to the report, I was shot five times. One of the bullets landed about one centimeter from my heart. During transport in the helicopter from to the aircraft carrier to the hospital in Germany, the bullet shifted and my heart stopped. The medic was able to bring me back, but they honestly didn't think I'd survive the surgery. And they also had to deal with my head injuries."

"How did you get those?"

"The spin was so violent that when we ejected, we both hit the casing of the cockpit. My injuries from that were worse than anyone knew, and I suffered a brain bleed and slipped into a coma. I guess I was out for about a week."

"Shit. That's bad."

"I was pretty fucked up. I spent another week in that hospital, but the first two days, all I could think about was how quickly would I be able to get back to work. I thought all I wanted was to get back up in the skies until the Navy showed me footage that they'd obtained from one of our drones. Not only am I lucky that I survived the aerial maneuver I had to perform to get out of the way of missile lock, but I'm lucky I was even able to remain conscious as long as I did. Hilltop, my copilot, passed out seconds after the spin started. By all rights, I should have died at least five different times that day."

"But you didn't."

"Nope." His chest puffed up as he took in a deep breath. He shoved his sunglasses up on top of his head and caught her gaze. "I also realized that while I loved what I did and I wouldn't trade in all those years as a fighter pilot, it was time to do something a little less dangerous."

"You Brotherhood Protector guys get shot at a lot."

He laughed. "Speaking of my job and bullets flying, I'm between assignments, and I'm pretty handy with a hammer. I thought I'd fix your place up so you can get back in business."

She shoved her empty plate aside. Her mother wasn't stupid. She wouldn't send Big Cal, or anyone else for that matter, right away. But that didn't mean she didn't have someone watching, lurking in the shadows, reporting back. For as long as Magnolia stayed and went about life as business as usual, her mother wouldn't do anything crazy. "We need to talk about that."

"Okay," he said.

"I need you to help me with something."

"What's that?"

"I want you to help me with a new identity and to go off-grid. I overheard you talking to that Dakota guy about his wife and what she went through with the underground this morning."

"That's for battered wives and children. You don't meet the criteria." He cocked his head. "And I don't appreciate people listening in on my phone calls."

"I didn't mean to, honestly. But you mentioned my name, so my ears perked up. I assume that's who you meant when you know people."

"I can't get into that and the underground isn't the place for you," he said.

"If you won't hook me up, I'll go searching on my own."

He leaned across the table and took her hands. "Running from your mother isn't the answer." He pressed his finger against her lips when she tried to argue. "I will make some inquires on how to do it right, but only on one condition."

"What's that?" she asked.

"You stay here with me until and let me protect you until either I'm forced to get you a new identity, or this is over."

She didn't have to think twice about her answer. "Deal."

DEWEY WIPED the sweat from his brow with a bandana before taking a swig of his water. One of the things he loved about Montana was the fact it was almost never humid and the only reason he was even perspiring was because he was desperately trying to keep Magnolia out of his mind.

But that proved impossible.

The idea that she could disappear out of his life forever made his heart hurt in a way he'd never experienced. He'd never really been all that great with women, but being a fighter pilot by itself was a great pickup line when he felt the urge. However his passion had been flying. His desire locked up in his career. His only real relationship had been to the Navy. He'd dedicated his life to serving his country, and he'd been happy to spend his days with his brothers-in-arms.

Now that he'd had a couple of years to adjust to civilian life, which hadn't been easy, he wanted something different.

He wanted flesh and blood to share his life with. Not a hunk of metal and a powerful motor. However, now that he'd successfully changed course, he hadn't a clue as to how to go about it. Planes were easy. He knew how to fly them. He knew what they needed and when. He didn't have to think about it. Women, on the other hand, were aliens to him, and he hadn't a clue as to what made them tick.

Especially someone like Magnolia.

The sound of tires crackling across broken pavement caught his attention. He pushed open the door and waved to Maddog and Dakota.

He'd barely had a chance to formulate a plan, but what few thoughts he'd come up with, he ran them by Maddog and Dakota, as well as copying his boss, Hank Patterson, in on the conversation.

Magnolia had made it easy for him by officially hiring him, but he'd had to do some fast talking with Hank and their rates, offering to cover the difference. Wouldn't be the first time someone on Hank's payroll took on either a freebie or a client at a reduced rate, but Hank didn't like that Dewey didn't want to tell Magnolia about his generosity.

Something told him that she'd be offended by the gesture, and he just couldn't have that. He knew she struggled financially, and he had the money, so he might as well put it to good use.

"What are you two doing here?" he asked as he perched himself on a big rock between the house turned business and apartment and the parking lot.

Magnolia's shop was about a mile outside of town. Before she moved in and made it her tattoo parlor, it had been rented to one passerby after the other. It wasn't much of anything, but Magnolia certainly spruced it up and made it her own.

"We thought we'd stop by and give you an update on what we've found in person," Maddog said. "You should know that Hank is putting limited resources on this, unless we get a red flag."

"I figured as much," Dewey said.

"I wanted to talk to you about her options in the future, if it comes down to that." Dakota slipped from the passenger seat of the truck and leaned against the hood. "It would be good to get the ball rolling."

"I don't want her to know that." Dewey took a hefty swig of his water.

"Why not?" Maddog asked.

"Because I don't trust that she'd take the information and run out in the middle of the night. She just wants to be done with it, and honestly, I don't blame her, but I don't think it's the right thing to do."

"I agree," Dakota said. "But I've a go on getting her to the underground if we need to."

"I appreciate it," Dewey said.

"Big Cal is back in South Carolina, and we've got some friends keeping an eye on him and his known colleagues," Maddog said. "We'll know if he, or anyone he's associated with, heads in our direction."

"That's great. But what I really need is to figure out a way to break up Flower's new business dealings and have her busted for it before she's ever released from prison."

"That's going to be impossible." Maddog folded his arms across his chest. "Flower's lawyer managed to get the hearing moved up. She could be released next week."

"Our best bet is to let her bring these assholes to our doorstep where we can control the situation, gather evidence with the help of law enforcement we know and trust." Maddog held up his hand. "And yes, that means using Magnolia as bait. It's the only way."

"That's going to push her out the door faster." Dewey glanced over his shoulder, making sure she wasn't in earshot. While he worked on fixing the holes in the lobby, she went upstairs to pack up some of her things to take back to his place. He didn't like the idea of making her a sitting duck, but he also understood that business as usual meant they got to keep an eye on mommy dearest, as Magnolia called her, while they gathered intel and worked with locals and the Feds to bring down her mother once and for all.

"You're going to have to find a way to bring her on board," Maddog said. "Use that charm of yours."

Dakota laughed. "My daughters want to teach Dewey how to talk to the ladies."

Dewey shook his head. He'd been harassed by his buddies about Magnolia for months. He'd used her age as an excuse for his shyness. Or maybe it was his inability to commit to something with a heartbeat. It didn't matter. They were all just a means of alluding his fears of being rejected.

"He doesn't have much game," Maddog said.

The sound of the front door caught his attention. He glanced over his shoulder just as Magnolia dropped a suitcase and a large backpack on the front stoop. "I have one more suitcase and a duffel bag I want to bring to your place."

"If you haven't brought them downstairs yet, just leave them. I'll take care of putting them all in my truck," he said.

She nodded. "I've got my room all set up when you're ready for me to work on that tattoo of yours."

"I just need a few more minutes with my buddies."

"Whenever you're ready." She turned on her heel and disappeared into the lobby.

"What the hell is going on here?" Maddog lowered his chin. "Is she moving in with you?"

Dewey pushed from the rock. "It's the best way for me to protect her, so don't go reading into it."

"But she's packing most of her things," Dakota said. "Either she plans on running, or she plans on spending some time in your bed."

Oh, how Dewey hoped it was the latter.

CHAPTER 3

"How's your back feel?" Magnolia set two plates on the outside patio table. She wasn't the best cook in the world, but she did this one lemon and garlic chicken over chickpea pasta dish well.

"It's the same as it was when you asked a half hour ago." He topped off their wine glasses. "You really didn't have to cook. I could have done that."

"It's the least I could do," she said, tucking her hair behind her ears. "I'm going to demand that you let me help out around this place while I'm staying here."

"Just clean up after yourself," he said with a chuckle. "And I promise I'll try to remember to put the toilet seat down."

"Excuse me?"

He shrugged. "I've heard my married buddies and their wives fight over that, and I never thought in a million years I would ever have anyone to say that to, and I just thought it would be funny. Weird, but laughable."

"Whatever floats your boat."

"This is really good." He pointed to his plate with his fork. "I've never had anything but regular pasta before. I have to admit, I was a little worried."

"Wait until you try my cauliflower mash with bacon and sour cream."

"I hate cauliflower."

"You won't even know that's what you're eating, trust me." She took a sip of her wine. "But I should warn you, I only have like six or seven things I cook well."

"Not to brag, but I'm an excellent cook. We can share the duties, and I'll teach you what I know."

"Fair enough." She dug into her food, impressed by the flavor. It was always hit or miss since she never followed directions. She read them and then just did whatever she felt like. Her meals never tasted the same twice. Maybe now she'd actually write down exactly what she did and follow it for the next time.

Where the fuck did that come from?

Dewey had turned her world upside down, and if she were being honest with herself, it had nothing to do with what happened with Big Cal or her mother.

No. Dewey had gotten under her skin long before yesterday. But there was a plethora of reasons on why she'd never pursued him, and now that she would be staying under the same roof, what was stopping her?

Mother dearest and her fucking boyfriend, that's who.

"I need you to give me a copy of your schedule so that I can either be at the shop with you or have someone there until I can finish installing the security system."

"I feel horrible putting you out like this."

"You're paying me, remember."

"Not very much. I don't know how you and your buddies can stay in business with those rates."

"I told you, it's not the full rate because it's—"

She covered his mouth with her palm. She didn't feel like hearing his explanation again. Nothing he could say would make her believe anything other than he'd slashed his rate. And because of that, she wouldn't go sneaking out into the night. She owed him the opportunity to make things right for her, as long as he continued to work on plan B, just in case his idea went to shit. "What did Dakota have to say?"

He rubbed his forearm. "It's getting a bit nippy out. Why don't we go inside?"

"You're not going to avoid my question."

"No. I'm not. But I need to talk through some things with you first. We need to be on the same page."

"I don't like the sound of that." But once again, he was doing her so many favors, he at least deserved for her to hear him out. She helped him clear the table but insisted on doing the dishes while he lit a fire in the family room and prepared a sweet strawberry and cream dessert to go with some more wine.

It still amazed her that some woman hadn't gotten her hooks securely fastened into him and a wedding date set. He was the catch of the county; that was for damn sure. So, why had no one snatched him up? What was wrong with him? That was the million-dollar question.

Of course, she brought a shit ton of fucked-up things to the table, so being with him would be a stupid mistake.

However, if he made a move on her, she wouldn't pass up the opportunity.

What did that say about her?

She pushed the dishwasher closed, found the ointment she'd given him to protect her precious art on his back, and made her way to the family room, taking the glass of wine he offered.

He dimmed the lights. The fire crackled, creating a romantic ambiance that would be hard to fight. Not that she'd fight him all that hard. Hell, all he had to do was kiss her and she'd be putty in his hands. She wouldn't turn him down, and she was seriously contemplating making a pass at him.

"Lift up your shirt." She waved the tube of cream.

"I barely used that the other two times." He shifted, pulling the fabric over his shoulders.

Taking a generous amount, she rubbed her palms together before splaying her hands over his supple skin. His firm muscles twitched under her touch. She wanted to press her lips against his neck right under his earlobe. The thought sent a hot shiver from her nipples to her toes. "There you go," she whispered.

"Thanks."

She leaned against the sofa, crossing her ankles, letting her arm press against his strong frame. "So, what is this page you want me on?" She'd never wanted a man as much as she wanted Dewey. She knew he'd forever ruin her for any other man that might follow, and she didn't care. She'd never marry. She'd never have one man in her life long term. Having kids was a pipe dream. She wasn't sure she could be a good mom, considering the stock she'd come from. Genetics played a huge role in any person's ability to parent, and her family tree left something to be desired. It wouldn't be prudent to procreate.

"For the most part, my organization specializes in keeping people safe, but we often take matters in our own hands when it comes to justice."

"What does that mean?" she asked.

"Simply put, we don't want your mother back on the streets, so we're doing what we can, using the resources that we have, working with both local and federal law enforcement to make sure she and her crew are cut off at the knees."

"I don't think I like the direction of this conversation."

"We made a deal, remember?"

"I do. I just never planned on keeping my end of the bargain."

He arched a brow. "At least you're being honest."

"I need that bitch out of my life for good, and the only way I see that I can do that is for me to change who I am."

"I know that's what you think, but trust me, you'll still be looking over your shoulder, wondering if she's figured it out. You'll never be truly rid of her until you can be sure she can't come after you ever again, and that won't be until you're sure she can't reach out from either prison or the grave to fuck with your life. Right now, she can still do that. Give me and the Brotherhood Protectors a few weeks, and we'll rid her from your life for good, letting you stay here in Montana where I believe you want to live. You've set up roots here, haven't you?"

"Is that what you want? For me to have a life here?"

"Would that be so horrible if that's what I wanted?" He reached out and palmed her face, fanning his thumb across her cheek.

"No." She curled her fingers over his wrist. Since she'd left South Carolina, she'd never done a single reckless thing. She kept her head down, worked her craft, and did her best not to make waves. What few relationships she had with men, they'd been with the kind of dudes who couldn't, or wouldn't, become emotionally attached.

And she certainly only went after the kind of men who were the love 'em and leave 'em brand. She never had her heart broken, and she doubted she'd left any bloodbaths behind.

It worked for her.

But the last year, all she could think about was Dewey, but he didn't give her a second thought, except for her mad skills to ink his body.

Or at least that's what she thought, and it had been for the best because he was the one that would make her bleed out.

"But since when are you interested in me? Why now?"

"I've always liked you."

"That's not what I asked." She really didn't understand why she needed clarification, other than maybe the need to put parameters on whatever was going to happen between them, because while she knew the people he worked with were good at their jobs, she didn't believe for one second any of them would be able to stop her mother.

"Would you like me to be brutally honest?" he asked.

"I'd prefer it."

He leaned in, giving her a short but sweet kiss. He

took her hand in his massive one, holding it tenderly. "I'm forty."

"Yeah, so?"

"And how old are you?"

"Twenty-seven." She leaned her head back and stared at the crackling fire. "I forget how young I am sometimes. I've seen more in my first eighteen years than most do in their entire lifetime."

"I'm sorry," he said. "I can't imagine. My childhood was almost literally unicorns and rainbows. I think that's why I chased the adrenaline high so much."

"I suppose it's why I like wide open and quiet spaces where nothing happens." She turned her head, catching his gaze. "Is my age the only thing that stopped you?"

"It's the excuse I used because I'm afraid."

"Of me? Why?"

"Imagine being my age and the last real girlfriend you had was when you were twenty. I look back over my life and I don't even think I've ever been in love, other than with my planes. Because I like you, I didn't know how or what to do. I felt like a stupid kid, and then when I watched some asshole shoot up your place and drive off, I couldn't sit the sidelines anymore." He jerked his head back. "Why didn't you ever come on to me?"

"Before I answer that, I need you to be truthful with me about something."

"All right."

"If, by the time my mom gets out of jail and starts sending her crew here, or she heads here, will I be able to disappear?"

He closed his eyes for a long moment before blinking them open. "Dakota and his friends are working on it. They will make sure you'll have a new identity set up if we need it. I promise you that will be ready at the snap of a finger if we can't take your mother and Big Cal down."

She pressed her mouth over his, slipping her tongue between his lips. He tasted like the dew on a warm summer morning. "I always told myself if you asked me out, I'd go, but I'd never make the first move."

"Why?"

"For a really smart guy, you're kind of stupid." She tapped his temple. "You're the kind of man I could fall head over heels for." She snapped her fingers. "It was hard enough sneaking out of your bedroom window before I ever even kissed you; imagine what it's going to be like when we have to say goodbye either because my mother gets out or she kills me."

"I'm not going to let either of those things happen."

"You can't guarantee that any more than you can't promise we won't end up breaking each other's hearts."

The old saying that *it was better to have loved and*

lost than to have never loved at all played over and over in her head. She would forever dream about Dewey; she might as well have a tangible memory to hold on to, as selfish as that might be. Throwing caution to the wind, she tossed her shirt to the side and straddled him, pressing her mouth over his as she grappled with his shirt, desperate to feel his skin.

Panic gripped her gut. Her pulse pounded in her head. She'd always been a little shy when it came to sex, but she managed. However, she was all of a sudden painfully aware she was about to get naked with Dewey. Her insides rattled like tree branches rustling in forty mile-per-hour winds.

Masterfully, he lifted her into his arms as if she were a feather and carried her into the master suite. He pulled back the comforter and laid her down on the bed, fluffing the pillows under her head. Standing at the edge of the bed, he pulled his shirt over his head and undid his belt buckle. "I have a condom in the nightstand."

"I'm on the pill. I haven't had sex in almost a year." She licked her lips in anticipation. Her eyes soaked in every glorious inch of his long, lean muscles. She heaved in one heavy breath after the other as he slowly lowered his jeans over his hips, shoving them to his ankles.

"I'm clean, so no condom it is." He leaned over, kissing the center of her stomach while he tugged at her shorts, easing them slowly over her thighs. His lips and warm tongue traced a path down her belly.

Gripping the sheets, she swallowed her breath. "Oh, God," she said with a throaty moan. She fumbled with the front clasp of her bra. She didn't really have much of a need for the undergarment, but she once had a teacher in high school tell her that no matter the size, gravity eventually would catch up to her, and since that day, she always wore one without fail.

He slipped a couple of fingers inside.

She arched her back, digging her heels into the bed. "You go right for the prize."

"The prize was more than ready." He pulled his fingers out and plopped them into his mouth. "Does that bother you that I went right there?"

"No." She blinked wildly, trying to focus on his sexy half-smile as he stroked her a few times before licking his fingers again. "Do that again but this time, let me taste myself." Did she just say that? It wasn't like she'd never kissed a man after they'd gone down on her, but she'd never asked them to share her flavor.

He palmed her, rubbing her hard nub as he caressed her insides. Raising his hand, he slipped his index and middle fingers into her mouth, holding her gaze. He licked his lips. "You're a wicked woman."

"You're bringing it out in me."

He continued to toy with her, teasing her with his

fingers before leaning over and spreading her with his tongue.

"Oh, my God," she whispered, lifting her hips, trying not to grind against his mouth. Having an orgasm wasn't the easiest thing for her to do with a partner. She had no problem giving one to herself, but with a man? She could count the number of times on her right hand. So, she'd become the master at faking it.

But she didn't think she'd have that problem with Dewey.

If anything, she might have a different kind of problem.

He did things with his tongue that wreaked havoc on her entire system.

She gasped for air, but her lungs burned. A wave of heat coated her skin like a lazy river winding through the mountains under the scorching sun. Her toes curled and she lost all control. "Dewey," she cried out. Tossing her head back and forth, a climax so powerful tore through her, and she thought she might flip herself right off the bed.

He flattened his hand on her belly, still rolling his tongue gently over her, slowing his motions. His lashes lifted, showing off his lust-filled eyes. "Are you always so explosive?"

She opened her mouth to answer, but all that came out was another groan as he continued to tease her with his hands. She swallowed. "Not with men."

He lowered his chin and raised a brow.

"That didn't come out right."

Lowering himself on top of her, he took her mouth in a hot, wet kiss. "Are you telling me that doesn't happen when you're with other men?"

"That would be a good assumption."

"I don't know if I'm insanely proud of myself or horrified that you've had such terrible lovers."

"I don't think it was them, but more a me problem," she managed between ragged breaths. "The timing is probably all wrong for this conversation."

In a tender moment, he kissed her nose. It was a sweet and loving gesture, and it took her breath away. "If I hadn't figured out what made you come, I would have asked what you liked. Didn't your previous lovers?"

No man had ever taken the time to find out what she wanted when it came to sex, but they certainly let her know what their fetishes were and had no problems demanding them. If she were being honest with herself, it was easy to get lost in whatever they wanted, forgetting about herself. "I can't say anyone ever did."

"That's a real shame." He pinched and twisted her nipple. "So, why do you think you're the problem?" He took his index finger and drew a circle with it around her nipple.

"It's hard to talk while you're doing that."

He chuckled. "I'm just getting to know your

body." He kissed her shoulder. "I would really like to know why you think that it's your issue that you haven't been able to have an orgasm outside of giving yourself one."

"For a guy who took a year to ask me out, you're not acting shy now." She took in a deep breath for courage. "My first real boyfriend was someone on my parents' crew. He was actually a young man whom my dad adored. But he was a selfish prick, and our sex life consisted of me learning how to fake it while creating new designs in my head." While she told Dewey her sad tale, he continued to tease her body with tender touches that made her wonder if this was close to what love felt like. The connection between her and Dewey couldn't be explained for two people who only knew each other on a surface level, but their bond cut deep.

"He didn't force you, did he?" Dewey asked.

"No. It wasn't like that. He was just selfish and only cared about himself when it came to everything, but when it's your first experience and you're as young as I was, you don't have a comparison."

"What about other relationships?"

"I've only been able to do that with one other man, and it took more concentration and work than it was worth, and when it was over, he decided he was done with me."

"I want to say you have shitty taste in men, but then I don't want to lump myself in with those assholes." His hands shamelessly roamed her body, finding every sensual spot. He left no part of her untouched.

Growing passion filled her soul. She cupped his cheek. "You're like no one I've ever met before."

He lowered his head, cupping her breast and raising it to his mouth.

She sighed.

"Since you've been satisfied, we can stop right here."

"Oh, no." She slipped her hands into the elastic of his underwear and finding his length, she curled her fingers around him, squeezing.

He groaned.

Pushing him to his back, she dotted his chest with kisses, scraping her teeth over his nipples, enjoying the way his body tensed. She yanked his boxers to his ankles and tossed them to the end of the bed. She wasted no time taking him into her mouth.

"Now who's going right for the prize." He ran his fingers through her hair.

She blinked her eyes open and paused for a brief second, catching his watchful gaze. It dawned on her that she had no idea how to please a man. Every guy she'd been with would just shove her head toward their cock and tell her to suck. About the only direction she'd received was to either use a little less or a little more teeth.

"What do you like?" she asked.

"Exactly what you were just doing."

"Like this?" She licked the length of him, squeezing his balls.

His lids fluttered as he groaned. His chest rose up and down as he took in quick breaths. "Oh yeah."

Giving a blow job had never been so exhilarating and empowering. She continued to tease him with her hands and mouth, keeping her gaze locked with his, enjoying how his eyes widened and then narrowed depending on what she did.

He never once pushed her head down on him, but he did gently fiddle with her hair. "Come here."

She crawled across the bed, lying down next to him.

Wrapping his arms around her, he pulled her tight against his chest and kissed her.

Hard.

He reached between her legs.

"Oh, God." Her body immediately responded to his touch, which surprised her. She'd been turned on the entire time, but she hadn't expected to have the kind of reaction that could bring about a second orgasm. She tried not to think about it. She couldn't put that pressure on herself because if she did, it for sure wouldn't happen.

"Relax," he whispered into her ear, rolling her on her back. He nestled himself between her legs, rubbing his thumb over her hard nub and pressing his stiff cock against her, slowly entering her inch by glorious inch.

She bit down on her lower lip. Her nipples throbbed. Her muscles twitched. Her mind emptied except for thoughts about Dewey and all the pleasure he brought to her body. Closing her eyes, she gave herself completely. "Dewey," she said with a moan. Her fingernails dug into his shoulder blades. She blinked, staring into his smoldering eyes as he picked up the pace.

Lifting her hips, she matched each thrust. "Yes," she whispered. The beginning of the first wave clenched her stomach. The anticipation of what was about to happen was almost as good as what she knew was coming.

"So beautiful," he murmured.

Just as his lips brushed over hers, a powerful climax tore across her body, smashing into her like a major tidal wave. She shuddered, jerking under his weight. Their tongues wrapped up in a passionate dance.

He pumped harder and faster until he stiffened, arching his back, his release exploding inside her, sending her into another round of convulsions.

She hugged him tight, wanting to feel all his weight. She buried her face in his neck. "I've never considered myself a prude, and even though I couldn't do that before, I still liked sex, but damn, I've been missing out."

He chuckled. "And to think, it took me over a year to ask you out. We could have been doing that all this time."

"You've never officially asked me out on a date."

He lifted his head and kissed her nose. "Magnolia. Next Friday night, would you like to go to a party with me?"

"What party?"

"A buddy of mine from the Brotherhood Protectors is having a barbecue at his place. I'd like you to be my date."

"Don't they have a thing against you dating your clients or something?"

"Not really. So? What do you say?"

"Only if you make that egg thing again."

He rolled to his side, pulling the covers over their naked bodies. "Deal."

She snuggled in next to Dewey, resting her head on his chest and her arm over his rock-solid abs. She took in a deep cleansing breath and let it out slowly.

Saying goodbye to him would be the hardest thing she ever had to do.

CHAPTER 4

DEWEY LEANED against the fence and nursed his beer, staring across the backyard of Clayton and Sage's house.

Magnolia had made friends with a few of the wives, but she tended to cling to Sage and Alabama, which didn't surprise him. Sage was close to her in age, and Alabama had been in the underground for almost a year before her ex-husband found her and nearly beat the shit out of her before Dakota had been able to get to her and their kids.

Dewey thought it might be a good idea for Magnolia to have a conversation with both Sage and Alabama, considering all the work they did with battered women, but now he was second-guessing that decision based on how intense that discussion seemed to be going. He worried Magnolia would continue to pressure him about the underground and what Dakota had planned. Dewey found it difficult to lie to her and if she asked him point blank, he didn't think he'd be able to keep the details from her regarding the undergrounds ability to whisk her away.

Thing was, he really only wanted to keep her close and with him for the foreseeable future.

Hank and Maddog strolled across the yard from the makeshift bar and headed in his direction.

"What do we know?" Hank asked.

"Not much," Dewey admitted. "She hasn't heard anything from her mother or Big Cal, and with Flower's court date moved up, we don't have much time."

"Well, we found something," Maddog said. "And I'd be shocked if Magnolia didn't know about it, so it begs the question: Why didn't she tell you?"

"Tell me what you found out and I might have an answer." Dewey didn't like being put on the defensive when it came to Magnolia. He also didn't like how some of his single co-workers were gawking.

He didn't wear jealousy well.

"So, you know they originally had her on murdering her own husband, but that was over-turned with new DNA evidence, and while they're pretty sure she hired a hit man to do it, they can't prove it," Maddog said. "But what we didn't know at the time was that she was also a person of interest in three other murders of her own crew."

Dewey's jaw slacked open. He'd never make it as a poker player. "I take it those are still unsolved?"

"Well, her dead husband was also a person of interest, and one spin on the story was that he'd been the one to kill them," Hank said.

"That actually makes sense if she then hired someone to knock off her old man in retaliation. Flower and Glenn had a pretty volatile relationship from what Magnolia has told me." Dewey polished off his beer. "When were the crew members killed?"

"Six months before Glenn was murdered," Hank said.

"That was about three years after she left. It's very possible she didn't know about the crew. She's tried like hell to forget about that part of her life," Dewey said. "She didn't know who Big Cal was, except for the tattoo he requested."

"Dewey has a point," Maddog said. "And up until last week, her mother hasn't bothered her in years."

"That's true, but I don't like how easily she found her." Hank folded his arms across his chest. "I also don't like that you told her she'd be able to disappear the second her mother is released from prison. If the Feds or the locals don't have anything on her, they're going to want to use her daughter and her ink talents."

"She won't agree to that." Dewey adjusted his shades to the top of his head. The sun had disappeared behind the mountain range, turning the sky a combination of dark blue, orange, and a wild purple color. "At least not right away."

"Are you playing her?" Hank asked.

"I wouldn't use that term," Dewey said. "And we can't, nor can the Feds force her to be some kind of an informant. If she wants to disappear, I'll help her."

"You do that, and you'll never see her again." Maddog slapped him on the shoulder.

"But it's what she wants and it means she'll be alive, I'm inclined to give it to her. Not to mention, it is her call." Dewey gagged on the words. A couple of days ago, he wouldn't have said them, but with every minute he spent with her, he realized he'd do anything for her.

Anything.

"You're right. It is her call, but we've just put some manpower into this, so I'd appreciate it if you at least try to talk her into it," Hank said.

"I will." And Dewey meant it. He desperately wanted her to stay, if only to find out if the wicked adrenaline rush he got every time she breezed past him was something that would end when the newness wore off.

Or if this was what it felt like to fall in love.

He smiled and nodded at Magnolia, holding up his empty glass bottle. "She wants her mother and Big Cal behind bars, but she also wants to feel safe."

"That's your job," Hank said. "I'm going to go find my wife."

"I should go find mine as well." Maddog stuffed his hands in his pockets and headed toward the barn.

Magnolia strolled across the yard, carrying two beers. She handed one to Dewey. "You all looked deep in conversation," she said in that sweet voice that turned his muscles to putty.

"I could say the same about you and the ladies."

"Sage and Alabama are really nice. I can't believe what Alabama lived through."

"She's a strong woman."

"You can say that again. But so is Sage in a different way."

Dewey nodded. "Let's go for a walk." He guided her around the barn and to a walking path that looped between a couple of the properties.

"Is something wrong?" she asked.

"I don't know," he admitted. "What do you know about your mother's past crew? The one after you left."

"Nothing really. I mean, she and my dad worked for someone else until I was about sixteen."

"Harlem Light. Your dad took him out."

"That's right. It was a bloody mess, and for a while, I was terrified to even leave the house. Harlem had some loyal people, but eventually my mom and dad turned on them."

"What happened between your folks?"

"My dad couldn't keep his dick in his pants, which constantly pissed off my mom, who wasn't faithful either, so I never quite understood that dynamic. But my mom didn't know my dad had a thing for men. He was bi, and my mom was disgusted by the whole thing. They would fight, threaten to kill each other in their sleep, and then I'd have to listen to them have wild crazy makeup sex. It was gross. But I couldn't tell you why Mother killed him. I didn't even know that until I saw it on the news."

"There were three other men murdered from your mother's crew, and both your parents were on the top of the suspect list."

"I didn't know that. When I started inking her people, I tried like hell to forget their names. I didn't put them on the books. I have no record of them anywhere. Hell, I didn't even get paid for them."

"That's rude." He stopped in a clearing and found a large boulder to sit on.

"I saved the money I got from the legit jobs I had between waitressing and my other clients. When I had what I thought was enough, I ran."

"There's something missing," he said, scratching the back of his head. "I know it makes sense that your mother would assemble a band of criminals, but I'm honestly struggling with why she wants you so badly when she left you alone for four years before she went to prison."

"She didn't really leave me alone. She threatened me all the time if I didn't come back. She'd email me regularly, tell me she'd find me and send someone after me and if I didn't do what she wanted, I'd pay the ultimate price, whatever that meant."

"But she never sent anyone after you. All bark and no bite." Dewey had dealt with a lot of scumbags over the years, and when they wanted something, they either got it or got rid of it. "Why do you suppose that is?"

"I gave up trying to figure out my parents a long time ago."

"We need to dig a little deeper because this doesn't add up." He took her chin with his thumb and forefinger. "I want you to do something. You're not going to like it, but I think it will help get us some answers."

"What's that?"

"I need you to reach out to your mother."

She batted his hand away, stood, and paced on the path in front of the rock. "Nope. No way. I'm not having any kind of communication with that woman."

"Right now, she's behind bars. She can't hurt you." He held up his hand. "I heard my mistake. Big Cal or someone else could come back, but you've got me and the power of the Brotherhood Protectors. Nothing is going to happen to you."

"Why do you want me to do this?" Magnolia planted her hands on her hips and glared at him. If her eyes were pistols, they'd be firing bullets right now.

"Two things stick out in my mind. First being Big Cal is just now getting your mom's tattoo and second is the fact your mother isn't contacting you, when in the past, it was always her, and I read some of those messages she sent you. I would think she'd want to drive that point home by contacting you personally."

"But she's in jail. Don't they read all her correspondence? Why would she risk something like that?"

"That is a good point."

"Also, she wouldn't want the man she's fucking behind my father's back to have her signature ink until after she had my father killed, but don't forget, she didn't think she'd ever get out of jail. Why come after me?"

"Because she can," he said.

She opened her mouth but made no sound.

"You agree that might make sense?" he asked. It was always difficult to watch someone grapple with the reality they tried to bury deep in the back of their minds, especially someone you care about. However, he needed her to understand that things weren't always what they appeared to be and that sometimes the boogeyman was someone else.

"I suppose."

"All I want you to do is reach out and tell her you got her message and you want to know when you can expect the next client. Tell her that your new boyfriend is with a private protection agency and is nosy."

"Boyfriend?"

"That is what I am, for the time being."

"I don't even know how to respond to that," she said.

Needing to feel connected to her, he took her mouth in a hot, commanding kiss. He pulled her tight to his chest, wrapping his arms around her body, holding her close. "I care about you," he whispered, "and I know you think you might have to leave, but I don't want you to. And until that time comes, if it comes, I want to be the only man in your life."

"You are," she said, palming his cheek. "I just didn't expect to hear the word *boyfriend*."

"Does that bother you?"

"No. But it's as unexpected as all the orgasms you've given me."

He laughed. "Shall I give you one right now?" Oh, how he loved to make her body squirm and hear all the little love noises she made. He couldn't care less about his own release. Hers was all that mattered. He slipped his hand between her legs, cupping her, rubbing gently, kissing her neck.

"Seriously?"

"Are you saying no?"

"No. I mean I'm not saying no." She spread her legs, giving him better access to her panties under her skirt. "This is so unfair."

"What is?"

"You've awakened something in me I can't control."

"I don't want you to. I want you to let go and just feel it." Carefully, he pushed her thong aside and slipped his fingers inside. She was wet and ready. Her body rocked against his motions. She held back nothing, giving herself freely. Anytime they made love, she took what she needed, and he expected nothing in return. She always gave as good as she got, but in this moment, he knew this would be all about her and that made him ridiculously happy.

She delivered the best.

And she should have an orgasm every time she had sex. It was a moral imperative. If he could give her one on a daily basis, he'd do it. She should be put on a pedestal and loved and admired because she was special in so many ways.

She gripped his forearms. Her breathing came in short pants. "You make me crazy."

"I hope in a good way." He rubbed her hard nub in a circular motion like he'd done the very first time they'd been together, dipping his finger in deep, stroking a few times before repeating the motion.

He smiled as her head dropped back and her thighs tightened around his hand.

She shuddered, jerking forward. Her nails dug into his skin as she called out his name.

A bird startled in the tree above, rustling the leaves as it flew overhead.

"How do you do that to me with just your hand and in like five minutes?" She let out a long sigh and nuzzled her face up against his neck.

He wrapped his arms around her body.

"I'd like to be a cocky asshole and say I'm a master at giving women orgasms, but this is all your body. I'm just doing what I've learned you like and what works." He took her chin with his thumb and forefinger, kissing her sweet, plump lips. "You're an amazing woman."

Her deft fingers found the button and zipper of his pants.

"Whoa. What are you doing?" he grabbed her wrist. "We should get back to the party."

"But you haven't had your turn."

He arched a brow. "We can be done."

She stood. Lifted her miniskirt and shimmied out of her thong, tossing it at him.

Things had already been a little tight inside his jeans. Now they bordered on painful.

Slowly, she unbuttoned her sleeveless blouse, showing off a white lacy bra with a front clasp that didn't remain closed very long.

A guttural groan vibrated in his throat. He stood, yanking her into his arms and assaulting her mouth. He'd never wanted anyone more. His desire cut through his heart right to his soul. "Turn around and brace yourself against the tree," he whispered in her ear. He probably wouldn't last any longer than she did.

The sun's rays reached down through the branches and warmed his already heated skin. He kissed her neck, inhaling her strawberry-scented shampoo as he cupped her tiny breasts, pinching and tugging at her nipples, pushing himself against her bare ass, trying to control his desperation.

He'd never be able to deny her anything, and that truly scared him, but not as much as losing her forever. Sucking on the tender spot of her neck just below her ear, he thrust inside her, holding her hips steady.

"Yes," she said with a sigh, pushing harder against him.

With every deep plunge, she rolled her hips, shifting the angle, making it impossible for him to maintain any kind of command over his body.

He stretched out one arm, gripping the tree trunk.

"Dewey, now. Please." She shuddered, dropping her head back. Her knees bent as her climax continued to roll from her body, stealing his release, taking it for her own.

He held her so tight in fear they both might topple to the ground.

In the distance, he heard a dog barking.

"We should probably get dressed before someone walks past. People do use this trail."

"Good idea." She smacked her lips against his cheek. "You've turned me into a slut."

"Don't ever call yourself that again." He hiked up his pants and went on the hunt for her panties. "But I'm not complaining."

"I would hope not." She tucked her hair behind her ears and smoothed down her skirt, but she still looked like a woman who'd just been thoroughly fucked. "Okay. I'll do it."

"Do what?"

"Contact my mother."

His heart stopped for a second. "I hope you don't think I did all that to—"

"Don't even say it." She looped her arm around his waist. "I know you better than that."

"Good."

She glanced up at him. "What's the status of my new identity?"

"It's not ready yet, but we could have you in the underground tonight if we had to." He kissed her forehead.

"You couldn't come with me, could you?"

"No." He probably could, but as much as losing her would kill him, he couldn't disappear, never to see his parents or brothers and their families ever again. He couldn't do that to them either. It wouldn't be fair.

Talk about being between a rock and a hard place.

CHAPTER 5

EVER SINCE MAGNOLIA sent an email to her mother, she'd been on edge, constantly looking over her shoulder. Dewey hadn't left her side since yesterday, and currently, he was finishing up painting the lobby. She should feel safe, and in a way, she did. She knew, deep down, Dewey would do whatever he could to protect her, but he really didn't know the lengths at which her mother would go to get what she wanted.

Magnolia, on the other hand, had seen it firsthand.

She adjusted the magnifying glass and pressed her pen against Dakota's skin. "Your children have some interesting names."

Dakota laughed. "My first wife's name was Lunar, so we thought River and Sky were good names for our girls."

"That is cute," she said. "It's interesting that you met and fell in love with a woman by the name of Alabama when you're also named after a state."

"Well, that's not my given name, nor is that hers," he said. "I'm originally from North Dakota, and it was a nickname that stuck. Alabama changed her name when she went underground. But our boys are really named Wyoming and Colorado. And if the next kid is a girl, her name will be Moon, and if it's a boy, we're leaning toward Montana."

"You know. Dewey nearly fell off his chair when he heard you were having another kid."

"Trust me. It wasn't planned. Neither was Colorado, but those are the best kind of surprises," Dakota said. "If you have questions for me, go ahead and ask. Before Lunar passed away, she did a lot of work with the underground. It was her passion. And you've spoken to Alabama about her experience running from her asshole ex-husband."

Magnolia finished the shading of the addition of his family tree. Many tattoo artists wouldn't work on a tatt that someone else had started, but for the men and women who were busting their asses to help her, she'd gladly do anything they asked. She pushed aside the light and set her pen down. "It's possible that I could be found."

"It is," Dakota said. "It's not likely. They work very hard to get rid of the paper trail. But we're dealing with humans and emotions, and when you leave people behind that you care about, it's really hard not to reach out."

"I don't have anyone." She tried to swallow her lie, but she coughed instead.

"What about Dewey?" Dakota arched a brow. "It's obvious to all of us he cares about you."

"He's a good man." She took a cleaning towel and wiped down Dakota's arm before putting some cream on it. "But contacting him after I disappeared would put him in danger. I couldn't do that to him."

"You do understand what we do for a living puts us in the line of fire on a regular basis."

She let out a long breath. "My mother is ruthless. I'm worried with this game we're playing that she'll hurt him anyway in trying to get to me. I feel like I'm in a damned if I do, damned if I don't situation."

"You kind of are," Dakota said. "The underground has helped a lot of women escape abusive relationships and start new lives when the system fails them. Both Alabama and I still believe in the courts and going through proper channels, when possible. It might not have worked for her, but the underground not only saved her life and brought her and Wyoming to me and my girls. However, if I'm being totally honest, I don't think it's the right move for you. Not at this juncture."

"You don't know what it's like to live your life constantly looking over your shoulder."

"I know. But my wife does and it's no way to live.

You go underground, that's not going to change. Ever." Dakota stood. "I know you think you need to leave the second your mom is released, but consider giving us and the Feds a little more time. If we think your mom is on the move to come after you, Dewey will take you to a safe house. We will protect you."

"I'll think about it."

"Good." He stood. "Now, what do I owe you?"

"This one is on the house for all the work you did fixing this place up. My landlord is thrilled, and no way could I have afforded it."

"That seems like a fair trade."

Her phone buzzed. She glanced at the cell. The number for the correctional facility her mom had been held at flashed across the screen. "It's my mother," she whispered, clutching her necklace.

"Dewey. Get your ass in here," Dakota yelled. "Answer it. Put it on speaker. I'll be right back. Don't say much."

She nodded, taking in a deep breath. She hadn't seen her mother in over seven years, and the last time she'd spoken to her had been when she'd found out her father had been murdered. That conversation hadn't gone well.

"Hello," she said just as Dewey came barreling into the room. He lifted her right off her seat and set her on his lap, holding her hand tight.

"I have a collect call from Flower Clarke, will you accept the charges?"

"Yes." A thick lump stuck in her throat. She sounded more like a frog.

"Magnolia? Are you there?"

"Hello, Mother," she managed to croak out.

"I have to say, I was shocked to hear from you." Her mother's voice sounded different. Softer. Nicer. And that made Magnolia's pulse race faster. Memories of when she'd been a little girl and her mother would climb into bed with her and read her a bedtime story flashed in her mind. She'd buried those images deep, not wanting to be reminded of the few good times she'd had because they'd been destroyed so easily. Her mother cared more about beating the system and hiding her money than she did her own flesh and blood. "But I'm terrified of the subject."

"What does that mean?"

"I'm not in contact with Big Cal. I haven't been in a couple of years," her mother said. "I'm not getting my crew back. That would be suicide, or at the very least, a ticket back into this hellhole, and I never want to see the inside of this joint again."

Dewey ran his hand up and down her back.

Dakota had pulled out a tablet and was tapping on the screen.

The air in her lungs deflated.

"I don't believe you," she said. "He had me put your crew tattoo on his shoulder, and then he told me he'd be sending more my way, and then he shot up my shop."

"Fucking asshole," her mother muttered. "Did you call the police?"

She glanced to Dewey for direction on what to say.

He found a pen and piece of scrap paper on the table and scribbled her a message.

"Yes. But I didn't give them all the connections."

"Well, maybe you should. Big Cal is dangerous," her mom said.

"So are you, Mother."

"You've always used that word with such disdain," her mom said with a long breath. "I know you have no reason to believe me or trust me, but I had nothing to do with whatever Big Cal said or did. He wants revenge on me."

Dewey wrote on the piece of paper.

Magnolia swallowed. "What reason does he have to get back at you for?"

"You don't want to know."

"He shot at me, Mother. I think I have the right."

"He's your biological father."

"What the fuck?" Magnolia bolted upright. "You've got to be kidding me."

"I wish I was, and I wish he'd never found out. But to make a long story short, once he did, he had your father murdered, and he was the one who set me up to take the fall. He destroyed my crew, killing my best men. And if what you're telling me is true, he's planning on making sure I end up back here and you end up six feet under."

"That's a big fucking tale, Mother."

"I fucking hate that you call me that," her mom said. "I know I deserve it. I know I'm a shitty person and was a horrible parent. When I get out of this place, I had planned on keeping my head down and doing whatever it took to live out my days like a normal person, knowing I'd probably never see you again. But I will be damned if I'm going to let that asshole touch you."

Magnolia gasped. Her head spun. Her stomach churned. She couldn't put together a coherent thought if she tried.

"Your father and I might have had a lot of problems, but Glenn was a decent man. He never hit me or you. We lived the kind of lifestyle that wasn't conducive to family life, and we made a lot of mistakes, but I wasn't the one who had your father killed. Big Cal is a mean mother fucker with a twisted mind. How he's stayed under the radar so long is beyond me."

Dakota lifted his tablet and showed it to Dewey.

Magnolia couldn't tell what was on the screen. She could barely see through the tears burning in her eyes. None of this made any sense. Her chest tightened, and she found it difficult to take a full breath.

"Flower, my name is Dewey. I'm a friend of Magnolia's."

"Okay," her mother said.

"No offense, but how do we know this isn't all bullshit to make Magnolia take her guard down against you?"

"I suppose you don't," her mother said. "I would suggest you call my lawyer."

"That's funny, Mother. Your lawyer's on your payroll."

"True," her mom said. "But the prison keeps records of everyone I talk to or receive communication from. While Big Cal has tried to contact me, I've not responded to him, and I won't. Not unless someone tells me it will help protect you."

Magnolia pushed from Dewey's lap and paced in a circle around the two men, gnawing on her thumbnail. Of all the things her mother was, a liar wasn't one of them. Of course she liked to fuck with you, but she didn't spin elaborate tales, not even to save her own ass. She'd been proud of who she was and what she'd accomplished in her life. She didn't care that she was a criminal.

For as long as Magnolia had lived under her parents' roof, they'd never killed anyone. Not with their own hands. They hired thugs to do that, but not very often. They ran a tight ship in their money laundering and counterfeiting business. They demanded loyalty from those under their employment and if you betrayed them, they turned their back. There was no forgiveness.

Her parents were deeply affected by those who opted to break their trust and force their hand, just never enough to stop their illegal activities.

Nope. That was more important than human life and much more important than the respect of their only child.

"Since when do you give a shit about me?" Magnolia placed her hands on her hips and stared at the phone.

"I've always cared, just not in the way a real mother should, I suppose. Besides, Big Cal isn't going to make this nice and neat. He'll torture you and anyone close to you."

"At least that's an honest answer," Magnolia mumbled, shifting her gaze toward Dewey.

He pursed his lips, shaking his head. "I'm struggling to believe any of this," he said. "Especially when we've spoken to the FBI who have a bug up their ass for you."

"Of course they do," Flower said. "They want me to give testimony against a couple of my ex-partners. And I'm guessing Big Cal has been slowly taking over their business. I've refused. I don't want to stick my head in that oven and have it explode."

"Have they offered you a deal?" Dewey asked.

"Of course. But I've already served my debt to society. If I give them all that I know, even if they put me in some kind of witness protection program, I'll be dead before I make it to the courthouse. That's not worth it to me."

Magnolia leaned against the back wall and folded her arms across her middle. Could all this be true? It was so far-fetched that she couldn't imagine that anyone could have made this shit up if they tried. She glanced between Dewey and Dakota who seemed to have some unspoken language going on.

"I need to do some checking into your story," Dewey said. "But what if I had another solution, one better than the Feds had, that would ensure your safety as well as Magnolia's and brought Big Cal down."

"I'd say tell me exactly who the fuck you are and then sign me up."

"We'll be in touch." Dewey reached out and ended the call. "Well, that was a strange twist of events."

"You can say that again." Magnolia swiped at her eyes. "My mother has this weird code about being honest. So much so that my father always told her when he cheated. He never lied about that. And she didn't lie to him. I did hear them once fighting over making sure I never found out the truth, but I was like eight. It was before they knew I'd figured out they were criminals. I didn't think it had anything to do with my paternity."

"What are you saying?" Dakota asked.

Dewey closed the gap, putting his arms around

her, hugging her to his chest. "You believe her, don't you?"

"Every fucking word."

"All right. Let us do some fact-checking and we'll go from there." Dewey tilted her chin. "It's going to be okay. We'll take care of it."

"I'm going to start with taking that call over to the office," Dakota said.

"You recorded it?" Magnolia asked.

"Almost every word. And then I'm going to have our buddies tighten their eyes on Big Cal. I'll be in touch in an hour or so."

"Thanks, man. I appreciate it." Dewey stretched out his arm. "You were her last appointment. We'll be at my place."

"Stay safe." Dakota disappeared.

She let out a puff of air. "I can't believe this is happening." She'd never been much of a crier. When she'd been young, her mother told her that strong women didn't cry, and especially not in front of a man. That was the one of two lessons she carried with her from childhood.

The other one she hoped she never had to use.

But right now, there was no stopping the flood-gates. She buried her face in Dewey's chest and sobbed. "I'm so sorry I brought you into this mess."

His hands roamed her back while his warm lips kissed her temple. "You forget, I just happened to be driving by."

"Why do you always make light of things?"

"My mom says it's because I'm afraid to feel too deeply. I used to think she was full of shit, but it's killing me to see you like this."

She tilted her head, tears burning a path down her cheeks. "You scare me."

"I should be offended, but I understand the sentiment because I'm utterly terrified of what's going on with us. After my brush with death and I came here, I put my heart and soul into my house. You should have seen it when I first bought it. Swear to God, it was falling over. Thing is, I kept telling myself it was time to settle down. I'd look around at men like Dakota or Clayton and I wanted what they had, but every time I saw you, I kept making up excuses, like I had to finish the renovations first."

"Or I was too young."

"Yeah. I've obviously gotten over that." He chuckled, but his face quickly turned serious. He ran his thumb over her cheek. "I'm falling in—"

"I'm not ready to hear or say those words yet."

He took her hand and pressed it against the center of his chest. His heart pounded so hard she thought it might bounce right out of his body. "I want you to know that I mean the words, even though it's difficult for me to say and you to hear."

"I know." She raised up on tiptoe and kissed him tenderly. "I'm hungry."

"Let's go home and grill some steaks."

That sounded so normal. And that's all she wanted. To live her life like the rest of the world.

Was that too much to ask?

CHAPTER 6

DEWEY TOSSED his extra helmet to Magnolia. "Are you ready?"

"Fuck no," she said.

He laughed. "Come on. It will be fun."

"If I was meant to fly, I would have been born with wings and feathers." She climbed on the back of his Harley, resting her hands on his hips.

For the last couple of days they did their best to remain positive and focus on the formulating game plan.

Dewey had always struggled with giving up control, one of the many reasons he'd become a pilot. He liked being in the driver's seat, but he'd learned in his career in the military and with the Brotherhood Protectors to trust the men and women working at his side.

"Is the mic on?" He flipped up the stand.

"I can hear you loud and clear."

He turned the key and revved the engine. "Now?"

"Yup."

"Here we go." While he would always prefer the sky to the road, being on his Harley, cutting through the fresh air at speeds that were slightly faster than recommended, though slower than what he'd done in his youth, was a decent replacement.

However, now nothing could take the place of the woman who had her arms wrapped around his waist. He understood her reasoning for not wanting to verbalize their love for one another. Perhaps it was too soon, too fast. And considering the circumstances, putting it on the back burner might be prudent. Yet, his heart ached to share his life with the only person who truly understood every aspect of who he really was and what really made him tick.

"You okay back there?" he asked.

"Can we just spend the day on the road?"

"You're going to find being in the sky exhilarating." He loved her so much, he was absolutely willing to let her go, but he would do everything in his power to make sure that was the very last option. Thus far, everything her mother had told them had proven to be fact. Magnolia didn't give a fuck who her father was, and Dewey understood why, which is why they weren't even pushing paternity. It wasn't smart anyway. Maybe in the future Magnolia would want to find out, and he'd support her, but for now, it didn't matter at all.

"I highly doubt anything could be better than this," she said.

He turned onto his favorite road that had twists and curves, making the ride to the small airfield almost as fun as a controlled stall, something he wouldn't do with her in the airplane for the first time. That would scare the crap out of her, and he wanted to get her back up a second time. Hell, he'd love to teach her to fly and share his passion.

"What's your favorite thing to do?" He down-shifted as he took the first tight corner. She leaned with him as if she'd been riding motorcycles her entire life.

"What do you mean?"

"I've only ever seen you create tattoos and read. What hobbies do you have? Interests that get under your skin." He'd been so busy enjoying her body that he couldn't believe in the last couple of weeks they'd been glued together at the hips that he hadn't taken the time to learn more about the love of his life. "Oh, and garden. I have no idea what you're doing in my yard, but it's looking beautiful."

"Thanks," she said. "I love art. That's pretty much my jam. But I've always wanted to ride a motorcycle. I've just never learned."

"This hog is too big for you to begin on, but we can get you a good starter one. I'd be happy to teach you," he said. "Have you ever been camping?"

"I lived at a few campgrounds when I first left South Carolina. It was a cheap way to live when I was often moving every couple of weeks or months. Sometimes I doze off in my hammock on the back porch. I love sleeping under the stars."

"Well, we'll take a couple of motorcycles, go up the mountains, and go camping."

"I'd like that," she said. "How come you don't have animals? It seems like everyone else in your organization has lots of horses, cats, and dogs."

"If it doesn't require fuel, I haven't a clue as to how to take care of it. I'd probably forget to feed them or something." He still felt that way about kids, but he figured if he ever found the right woman, he'd manage. Or at least he hoped he would. "Hang on tight. I like to take this corner pretty hard and fast."

"I like hard and fast."

He groaned. "I know." Leaning forward, he sped up. It seemed she had no problem being a little dare-devil on the back of a Harley. She should have no problem in his plane. The road twisted to the right and then took a ninety-degree curve to the left.

"Ahhhhh," she cooed as she tightened her grip. "Amazing."

"I love it out here." In the distance, a small jet

descended toward the runway. "And you're going to love it up there." He slowed as they approached the hangar where he stored his Skyhawk. It had been his very first purchase the second he retired from the military. It had terrified his parents, considering his brush with death had come in the form of a plane crash. While he no longer felt the need to test the limits of himself and his machines, he did like to get his blood pumping, just a little.

He rolled to a stop and shut down the engine. "I'm so excited I've got goosebumps."

"That's really fucking weird."

"Are you kidding? You're a virgin in flying in general. The only thing better than that is giving you an orgasm."

"You're obsessed with those."

"Damn straight I am." He undid the buckle on her helmet and took her by the hand, leading her toward the office.

"Does this operate like a regular airport?"

"Not even close. It's for small private planes, jets, a few charter companies, and lessons." He nodded and smiled at the person behind the desk as he signed in. He turned and pointed across the airfield. "Over there is the school I teach at." Two of the education planes had been pulled out of the hangar and were displayed proudly.

"You don't use your own plane?"

"Not usually, but I will when I teach you to fly."

"Let's stick with the motorcycle."

The sound of heels clicking against the concrete caught his attention. He glanced over his shoulder and rolled his eyes.

"Hey, Dewey." Hillary slinked across the floor wearing red pumps, a red tight-fitting dress with a matching red scarf. Her jet-black hair she'd pulled back into a ponytail and as usual, she wore way too much makeup. She was a pretty girl, but she tried too hard to be noticed. "How have you been?"

He looped his arm over Magnolia's shoulder. "Doing excellent."

"I didn't know you had a little sister," Hillary said.

Magnolia patted the center of his chest. "I'm not his sister."

"I see." Hillary jutted out her hip and folded her arms as she looked Magnolia up and down.

Wonderful. The last thing he needed was his ex-girlfriend with in a cat fight with his current one. What made it worse was that he'd read Hillary all wrong, and she still occasionally tried to change Dewey's mind. "Magnolia, this is Hillary. She's a flight attendant for a private charter company."

"Nice to meet you." Magnolia leaned closer to Dewey, slipping her arm around his waist. She slid her hand down his stomach and looped her finger into his front pocket.

He swallowed.

"So, she's your latest conquest." Hillary tapped her pointed shoe on the ground.

"I think you have that backwards," Magnolia said. "He's another notch in my bedpost. Now if you'll excuse us, I have a mile-high club I'd like to join."

Dewey tried not to chuckle, but it was impossible, especially when Hillary had an indignant scowl.

"Sorry to inform you, but you can't have sex while he's flying that little shitty plane of his."

"Hand jobs and fingers work just fine. Let's go, babe," Magnolia said.

"Your wish is my command." He turned on his heel, leading Magnolia toward his Skyhawk. "I can't believe you just said that."

"I can't believe you slept with a woman like that."

"We all make mistakes," he said. "And in my defense, when I first met her, she appeared to be a regular, down-to-earth chick. I had no idea her entire goal in life was to land someone from the Brotherhood Protectors. After three weeks, I'd had more than enough."

"I bet she didn't take that well."

He shrugged. "She moved on pretty quickly. And she's also given up on my type of man and is now into the rich cowboy, which is why she became a flight attendant for a private jet company. It's too bad because if she stopped trying so hard, she's not a horrible person, just very self-absorbed." He stopped in front of his pride and joy. "This is

Phoebe." He puffed out his chest and waved his hand out in front of him. "She's named after my only niece and the only girl in the family. She's quite the little princess and my poor brother has no idea how to handle it. It's funny as hell to watch, especially now that she's twelve and boy crazy." He pressed his hand against the nose of his white plane with the blue swirly stripe, his niece's name displayed on the tail, and smiled, which quickly turned to a frown.

Magnolia's face paled. She pointed to the prop, then turned and aimed her finger at the plane Hillary had stepped from. "That nice shiny one doesn't have that on the nose. That one is a jet. Yours isn't a jet?"

"Trust me, you don't want to be up in the air with me in a jet. At least not your first time."

"Well, let's do this before I turn around and run."

MAGNOLIA ADJUSTED the headpiece for the fifth time. As if that would make her feel better. "You do have a couple of parachutes in this flying lawn mower, right?"

"You know, I have a few buddies who like to do that for fun, and I just don't get why anyone would jump from a perfectly good aircraft." He stretched out his arm and flipped switches and pushed buttons. "Besides, the last time I did that, I died."

"That's not a funny. Not at all," she said shaking out her hands.

"Sorry. I shouldn't have said that. It's going to be fine."

Some person came over the speaker and rattled off commands.

"And away we go." Dewey patted her leg before he gripped what looked more like a handlebar than a steering wheel.

"You don't have to seem so excited." She didn't really have anything to grip, so she squeezed her thighs as the hunk of metal rattled.

The engine roared and the entire plane vibrated. It moved slowly at first, but it quickly picked up speed.

She bounced in the seat. Her heart pounded in her chest like a wild beast charging through the open prairie on the hunt for dinner.

"Are you doing okay?" Dewey asked.

"I'm still alive."

He chuckled. "The initial ascent is going to give you butterflies, but then it's going to feel like floating."

Filling her lungs with as much oxygen as possible, she held her breath and counted to five before letting it out slowly. She reminded herself that she was doing this in part because she truly wanted to get over her fear of flying, and because Dewey's eyes lit up like a kid on Christmas morning every time he talked about taking her up. It was too important to him which made it impossible for her to deny him this simple pleasure.

Realistically, she understood that she was safer in the air with Dewey than she was anywhere else in the world.

Why did she have to go and fall in love with him?

She'd never felt this way for anyone before, so she supposed she could be just infatuated with him, but every time she pictured her life anywhere other than Montana and without Dewey, she'd rather die.

"Whoa," she whispered as the nose bounced twice on the pavement. "Is that supposed to happen?" No sooner did she question that than the front of the plane completely left the ground.

"It's all good," he said, pulling the handles close to his chest. He glanced in her direction and winked. "We're flying."

"I see that."

She blew out a puff of air. The frogs jumping from her gut to her throat had calmed, but her pulse still raced wildly out of control. She leaned forward and looked down.

"I'm going to turn in that direction."

The plane dipped to her right. She gripped his leg in a knee-jerk reaction. "I think I just swallowed my heart."

He laughed. "I did that the first time I hit Mach five."

"I don't know what that is and please tell me I'm never going to find out."

"I can honestly say, you probably won't."

"It feels like we're sideways." Oddly, that didn't freak her out. Her crippling fear turned into exhilaration, just like he told her it would. Although, she still had some trepidation and knew that what goes up, must come down, but she didn't think she was going to toss her cookies anymore.

"We kind of are." He reached out across her body. "See that over there?"

"Yes."

"That's your shop."

"Seriously?" She covered the glare of the sun and squinted. "Oh. Yeah. So, your place has to be on the other side of town?"

"Actually, it's over there."

The plane leveled out as they headed to what she thought might be north, but she couldn't be positive.

"It's beautiful up here." She turned and smiled. "Thank you."

"I'm glad you're enjoying it."

"I wouldn't go that far, but I'm not hating it." Movement below caught her eye. "Oh, my. Look at the horses galloping through the fields. Their magnificent."

"Being up here gives you a very different perspective on life."

She couldn't take her eyes off the landscape below. "How high up are we?"

"Are you sure you want to know that?"

"I do." She pressed her hand against the glass window.

"We're only at about four thousand feet. I'm not allowed to go higher than ten thousand without a flight plan, but generally I stick to six or so."

"Where do you go?"

"Most of the time, I just go out for a joy ride, but sometimes I fly back to Knoxville to visit my parents. I've also taken trips to Dallas and Atlanta to visit my brothers, but not often."

"That's really kind of cool."

"Any place you'd like to go for a long weekend sometime?"

"You mean by plane?" She continued to soak in the sights. Everything looked so small, yet so spectacular at the same time.

"Yes. We could go to Salt Lake City or maybe Denver."

"Really? We could just hop in your plane and jet away just like that?"

He laughed. "Longer trips would have to be planned, and weather is a factor, but yes, we could."

"I think I could get used to this flying thing."

"That's my girl."

Suddenly, the aircraft jerked, and the engine made a sputtering noise.

Dewey pursed his lips and tapped one of the gadgets on the dashboard before glancing over his shoulder. "What the fuck? That can't be right."

"What's wrong?"

"You don't want to know," he mumbled. "What I'm about to do is going to scare the shit out of you, but I need you to remain as calm as you can, okay?"

She swallowed and nodded wildly as the plane dipped lower, to the left, and made a quick turn back toward the airport. Just as he did that, the engine sputtered again, before going dead silent.

"Mayday, mayday, mayday."

"This is the tower," a man's voice came over the speaker.

"This is Dewey Stone. I have engine failure. I need to do a deadlock landing, and I'm on course to overshoot the runway by two hundred feet at this glide."

"We've got eyes on you. Any other problems?"

"No," Dewey said. "Not that I can tell."

"How about a zigzag approach. That might cut the overshoot down by a hundred feet."

"I can do that."

Magnolia pressed her head back against the seat and practiced her deep breathing she'd learned at her one and only yoga class. She wanted yoga to be her thing, but she just didn't have the patience, which was weird, because as an artist, she needed to take things slow and be aware and sensitive to details.

She closed her eyes, but that just made her feel

sick to her stomach. So, instead, she opted to focus on Dewey. Wonderfully sexy Dewey. She glanced in his direction.

He held the handle in both hands. His lips were drawn tight together. His intense stare straight ahead.

"I've done a dozen deadlock landings. We're going to be just fine."

"I don't even know what that is."

"It's basically landing with little or no engine power," he said.

"I don't understand why we haven't fallen from the sky." It was eerily quiet without the roar of the motor.

"It doesn't work that way."

She wanted to ask him about his crash that nearly killed him but thought better of it under the current circumstances.

"However, this isn't going to be an easy landing. I'm sorry about that." He glanced in her direction. "I want you to put your head between your legs and brace yourself."

"How did this happen?"

"I have my suspicions, but let's talk about that once we're on the ground, okay?"

She nodded.

"Tower, this is Dewey. I'm approaching at 50 knots."

"You're still going to end up hitting the runway

late."

"I can pull back to 45 knots," Dewey said. "Trying to restart engine."

Magnolia hugged her legs as her stomach ended up in her brain. Never in a million years did she think her first airplane ride would end up in a crash landing.

"Negative on the restart. 40 knots. Nose is up."

It amazed her how calm Dewey's voice had remained. But it stunned her that she hadn't been crawling out of her skin or screaming at the top of her lungs.

"Brace yourself. We'll be on the ground in five, four, three, two…"

The plane hit the pavement and bounced.

And bounced.

And bounced again.

The sound of rubber skidding across the tarmac filled her ears like fingers on a chalkboard. Her body jerked forward as it quickly slowed until it bucked to a stop.

Dewey's hands came down on her back. "It's okay. It's over."

She bolted to a sitting position, pushing the headset off her head. She wrapped her arms around his strong body. She wanted to cry, but no tears formed in her eyes. "What happened up there?"

"I only have suspicions." He cupped her face. "We

need to disembark so I can take a look at my plane and check to see if I'm correct."

"Please tell me."

"I know Phoebe, and I know aircrafts and engines better than the back of my hand. They don't cut out the way that one did unless they were tampered with."

CHAPTER 7

MAGNOLIA SAT IN A FOLDING CHAIR, sipping a bottled water, with Sage and Alabama and watched as Dewey, his buddies, and a few men she'd never seen before checked out his precious plane. She pressed her index and middle fingers against her wrist. Her pulse still raged out of control.

"How many times are you going to do that?" Alabama rested her hands on her pregnant stomach with her legs crossed at her ankles. She'd kicked off her shoes and wiggled her toes in the cool Montana air. While Alabama had a breezy personality, she also had a hard edge. Her story was not only horrifying, but it continually conflicted with Magnolia's thoughts and what to do if and when the underground came through. "It's been hours since you've safely landed."

The really weird part was she wanted Dewey to

take her back up again so she could have the full effect from take-off to landing. Anything would be better than what she'd just experienced, but she'd survived. And flying had been one of the most amazing things that had ever happened outside of meeting Dewey.

Ever since he stepped foot in her shop over a year ago, her life had changed in small ways. She smiled wider when she saw him. Her heart fluttered faster when he waved to her in town. She'd started going to the places she knew he frequented just to get a glimpse. She never thought anything would happen; she just wanted to be close. He had a way of making her feel special during casual conversation, and that was something no one had ever done.

And in the last few weeks, he'd stolen her heart, and she wasn't sure she'd ever get it back.

The roar of a jet approaching filled her ears. She glanced to the sky. The private plane that Hillary worked for came into view in the distance.

"I'm not sure what was scarier. The engine failing or meeting Hillary," Magnolia said.

Alabama and Sage both burst out laughing.

"She's a piece of work," Sage said. "And here I thought I used to be the queen of shallow and spoiled."

Magnolia jerked her head back. "I can't ever see you being like that."

"Oh, trust me. I was ridiculously naïve and quite

full of myself until I met Clayton. He opened my eyes to the world and showed me that writing a check helped, but it wasn't enough. I had to learn to roll up my sleeves and get a little dirty. But I'm not sure there is anyone who can show her the error of her ways."

"It's too bad, she's not a horrible person," Alabama said.

"That's what Dewey said, but I don't believe it." Magnolia didn't have great instincts when it came to people, but Hillary had the same manipulative look in her eyes that Magnolia's mother always had right before she fucked someone over. It was hard to describe the subtle twinkle that flickered behind her mother's gaze, but Hillary had it. At first, Magnolia thought it was jealousy that triggered her reaction, but the more she thought about it, the more she realized it was the similarity to her mother's personality that had gotten under her skin.

"Why?"

"I have nothing concrete to base that opinion on other than the way she looked me up and down with her judgy eyes."

"She went after a few men in the Brotherhood Protectors, but not as aggressively as she did Dewey." Sage tilted her head, shielding her eyes, her gaze following the jet as it landed on the tarmac. "She didn't want to let him go. She went as far as to tell everyone she was pregnant when she wasn't."

"She did what?" Magnolia gagged on the sip of water she'd just taken. Dewey had left out that interesting little piece of gossip. She supposed it didn't matter, but still, it bothered her that he chose to keep that information to himself instead of sharing it.

"Oh yeah," Sage said. "It's funny now, but it wasn't at the time. Poor Dewey. He was so freaked out. At the time, I think even the mere thought of having kids gave him heart palpitations."

"How long ago was this?" Magnolia didn't know why she needed to know the time line. She knew Dewey waffled with the concept of being a father, but he was the kind of man who would step up if any woman he'd been with had gotten pregnant.

"They dated when he first moved here, so about two years ago." Alabama rubbed her stomach. "This is the first time you're meeting her? Haven't you lived here longer than that?"

"I have, but I don't get out much. I might have seen her around town, but she's not the kind of person I'd want to get to know," Magnolia admitted. "How did he find out she wasn't pregnant?"

"He demanded she show him the proof," Alabama said. "All while she kept trying to seduce him, trying to get pregnant."

Sage waved her finger in the air. "Then she cried miscarriage, and he wanted to see the medical records. She then went around trying to destroy his reputation. Because he was new to the area and he didn't defend himself loudly, she put a small dent in it, but not for long. Eventually, the truth came out. But since then, she's kind of had it in for Dewey and occasionally causes trouble for him."

"Now I'm confused." Magnolia rubbed her temples. "Why do you all think she's not a horrible person if she's been doing all these bad things to Dewey?"

"She's just very misguided, which is something I can relate to," Sage said. "I don't think her parents ever wanted kids, and when she was in high school, they bought her a house outside of town. She lived her with a housekeeper."

"That's horrible." Magnolia understood what it was like to be tossed aside by family. It didn't feel good, and it often left you looking for affection in all the wrong places. "Sounds like she just wants someone to love her."

"Agreed. But she certainly has a screwed-up way of going about it." Alabama patted Magnolia's hand. "And for the record, she hates tattoos on women. She thinks any lady who would scar her body has no class and no chance of landing a decent man. So, it wasn't just you being with Dewey that had her panties in a wad."

"Well, she can kiss my tattooed ass." Magnolia raised her water.

"I like the way you think." Alabama laughed.

"Dewey's tattoo looks great," Sage said. "And so does Dakota's."

Alabama rubbed her growing belly. "My husband is crazy. He actually said that after I have this kid, we should have one more so we have an even number."

"Six kids?" Sage shook her head. "I'm struggling with two. I don't think we're going for a third."

"I appreciate you both coming and sitting with me, but you don't need to leave your families in order to distract me." Magnolia really liked both Sage and Alabama. For the first time since she'd left South Carolina, she felt like she had friends she could confide in, and while she'd known them enough to shoot the breeze with them in town for over a year, it had only been in the last couple of weeks that they had become girlfriends.

And it opened up Magnolia's soul to something she'd been craving her entire life.

Family.

It might not have been blood, but it was a family she could choose.

"This is our life. It's what we signed up for when we got married," Sage said. "Many of us lived a different kind of hell before we got here, and we back each other up. We're family. Dewey is family. That makes you family."

"I've never really known what a real family is like. I was raised by crazy people."

Sage laughed. "My parents tried to pretend to be

good up standing citizens, and I was so naive I bought it hook, line, and sinker. Imagine my surprise when I found my entire life was a lie. Thank God Clayton watched me get in the wrong car and chased me down; otherwise, I'd be dead."

Magnolia lifted her sunglasses and focused on Dewey who looked deep in conversation with one of the men from the Federal Aviation Administration (FAA). "Dewey doesn't think the engine just failed. He believes someone fucked with it."

"That's a given," Sage said.

"The fact that Big Cal managed to figure out about Dewey's plane and that he would even take me up in it is all the more reason I need to disappear." Magnolia let out a long breath.

"I know you're really interested in the underground," Alabama said. "And they did right by me, but remember, they also sent me straight to Dakota. They knew he could protect me better than anyone."

"Did they think your ex-husband would really find you?" Magnolia asked.

"My ex was a pretty powerful man with a lot of resources. Yes. Eventually, they figured he'd catch up with me, even with all the careful planning. Had they not directed me to the one man who would know without a doubt just by looking at me and my son that I was on the run and why, I'd be a dead woman."

"You think I should stay, don't you?" Magnolia changed her mind on if she should stay or if she should run a hundred times in the last hour. When Alabama and her husband showed up after the crazy landing, she'd overheard Dakota tell Dewey the underground was ready for her any time. She hoped she wouldn't have to confront Dewey on that juicy piece of information. That would change her opinion of him slightly.

"I do," Alabama said.

"And know this," Sage added. "Dewey might be a bit of a showboat when it comes to his planes and motorcycles, but he's a humble man. He's not arrogant, at least not anymore. If he didn't believe he could protect you, he'd tell you to go." Sage wiggled her finger. "And shit happens. Clayton got shot and nearly died saving me."

"And I got my ass kicked saving my family," Alabama said. "There are no guarantees in life. But if you love Dewey, which I think you do and I'm pretty sure he feels the same way about you, fighting for your future is worth it."

Magnolia never thought about a future. Not really. She lived her life hoping that her past never caught up to her, but that wasn't much of an existence. She kept people at a distance, never really allowing anyone in.

Until now.

She didn't ever want to let that go.

Whatever the guys were doing with the plane, they must be done because some of the men were rolling it toward the hangar while Dewey, Clayton, and Dakota strolled in Magnolia's direction.

"Whoa," Alabama said. "This kid is kicking really early." She grabbed Magnolia's hand and pressed it over her swollen stomach. "I felt my other two pretty early, but not this early." Her belly jumped.

"Holy shit." Magnolia shifted in her chair, moving closer and pressing her hand harder. "That's wild."

"This is my third pregnancy, and you'd think it'd be all like old news, but it brings tears to my eyes every time." Alabama fanned her face. "Don't tell my husband, but he can have as many kids as he wants out of me. I love this."

"Maybe you have two in there," Sage said.

"Oh, that would make my husband so happy," Alabama said. "And I do have built in helpers with my girls."

"Hello, ladies," Dakota said. "I take it that bundle of joy of mine is doing a tap dance."

"You can say that again." Alabama took her husband's hand and stood. "These crazy ladies were just talking about how interesting it would be if I were having twins."

Dakota coughed. "Are you?"

"Not that I know of, but we have the ultrasound next week. You never know," Alabama said. "That would give you the even number you want."

"But two at the same time? I don't know if I can handle it."

"If it's twins, you won't have a choice." She waved. "Later, girls."

"We're out of here too," Clayton said. "Our babysitter is about at her limits with our crazy rug rats. They take after their mother."

"Right," Sage said, shaking her head. "We'll talk soon." She leaned in and kissed Magnolia's cheek. "I think I want to get a tattoo."

"My prim and proper wife is going to ink her body." Clayton arched a brow. "Now that *is* sexy."

"Wait until you hear what I want and where I want to put it, old man," Sage said.

"I love it when you talk dirty." Clayton waved his hand over his head. "Watch your back, Dewey. And stay in touch."

"You know I will." Dewey plopped himself down in the chair, stretched out his legs, and crossed his ankles. "Thanks for coming out."

An aircraft similar to Dewey's taxied down the runway, picking up speed, which awakened the butterflies in her stomach. Even in the madness, she loved being in the air with Dewey.

He took her hand and stared at their intertwined fingers for a long moment. "I need to tell you something."

"Okay."

"The underground has a temporary placement for you if you want it."

Wow. She hadn't expected him to lead with that.

To the contrary. She anticipated him potentially not telling and once he did, trying to talk her out of it right off the bat; instead, he just tossed it out there for her to mull over.

He took her water bottle and brought it to his lips, taking a long draw. "It really is up to you. They will do the best they can to make sure you're safe. Obviously, I didn't do my best today."

"Did we crash? Did we die?"

"Well, no."

"Then I'd say you did right by me."

"I should have seen that my plane had been tampered with. I didn't do a thorough enough check."

She moved her chair close, facing him. "I watched you do your checklist. You actually asked me to be quiet and not distract you."

"I still missed it."

"You're really hard on yourself."

"I'd never forgive myself if something happened to you on my watch."

She pushed from her chair and climbed onto his lap, eyeing Hillary as she descended from the jet that had landed a bit ago. Magnolia had never felt the kind of passion that made a person need to mark their territory, but that's exactly what she was doing when it came to Dewey.

And not just for Hillary's sake. Anyone looking on, Magnolia wanted them to know that he cared for

Magnolia in a way he hadn't cared for any other woman before.

Even though she was going to break his heart.

And her own.

He wrapped his arms around her waist. "Big Cal's going to keep gunning for us."

"What do you think I should do?" One way or the other, she needed to hear his opinion. "And I want you to be honest. Please don't lie to me."

He leaned over and brushed his lips across her in a sweet and loving kiss. "Total honestly?"

"Yes."

"I love you," he said softly.

She inhaled sharply. Why did he have to say that? It wasn't going to make this any easier. "That wasn't what I was asking."

"I beg to differ." He wiped the single tear that burned a trail down her cheek. "My feelings for you go hand in hand in what I think is best for both of us."

"And what is that, exactly?"

"The underground does great work, but you'd have to change everything about who you are. You couldn't be a tattoo artist."

Her jaw slacked open. She hadn't thought about that.

He reached out and traced one of her designs on her shoulder. "You'd probably have to have some of those removed. I know they'd take care of you, but even with what happened today, I think I can do a better job, because I love you. However, if you feel safer leaving Montana, and me, behind, I love you enough to let you go."

She cupped his face. "You sound like a cheesy made-for-television romance."

He chuckled.

"When I climbed up on your lap, I did so for two reasons. First one was to make the bitch heading our way jealous."

"She's seeing red, I'm sure."

"The second was to say goodbye."

He opened his mouth, but she hushed him with her finger. "You changed my mind."

He arched a brow. "I didn't mean to do that. It's always your choice. I didn't tell you I love you because I'm trying to manipulate you. I just didn't want you to go without knowing how you've changed my life. It's really not meant to pressure you. Either choice is a good one."

"I know that." Her life had been a series of decisions based on other people. Even running from South Carolina, while it had been to save her own ass in the long run, she felt like she had no choice. If she'd stayed with her parents, she would have for sure ended up in jail or dead. This would be the first time she got to take a defining moment and determine which road to take. She didn't feel as though she was damned if she did, damned if she didn't.

Going underground had its own pros and cons as did staying, but it was her life. Her choice. "I love you too."

"That's nice to hear." He smiled.

"I know the underground and I know you and the Brotherhood Protectors will do whatever is necessary to keep me safe. I'm confident in that. But I'm not willing to give up who I am. Who I've become. Or what I feel when I'm with you."

His smile got wider. "The underground can keep everything on ice for you."

"Are you trying to get rid of me?"

"No. But we need to be realistic. Big Cal is still in South Carolina as is every person we know that works for him, so he's got someone out here that we don't know about."

"So what are we going to do?" she asked.

"I'll tell you after we deal with the lady in red." He patted Magnolia's bottom and helped her to her feet as he gave her a hot, wet kiss, swirling his tongue in her mouth. "That was a short run," he said to Hillary.

"We just had to picked up someone from the international airport," she said. "I heard what happened. That had to have been scary."

"Dewey handled it like the pro he is." Magnolia leaned into him. "Can we help you with something?"

"I just wanted to make sure everything was okay." Hillary pursed her lips.

"We're just fine, thanks," Dewey said.

"Actually, we're great," Magnolia added for good measure.

"I don't know why I bothered." Hillary turned on her heel and stomped off.

"Wow. You're jealous." Dewey hip checked her as they strolled across the pavement toward his Harley.

"No. I'm not." She swallowed. "I just heard what she did to you."

"Oh. Well. That was a long time ago. And until you, I've never trusted another woman to take care of birth control again."

She paused midstep. "Why'd you trust me?"

"Because having a child with you wouldn't be the worst thing in the world."

"Here you go." Dewey handed Magnolia her helmet and chuckled. "You look like you've seen a ghost." His phone buzzed. He pulled it out of his pocket and glanced at the screen.

Hank: Big Cal pulled a fast one and is missing.

"Fuck," Dewey mumbled.

Dewey: How the hell did that happen? Any idea where he is?

Magnolia tugged at his shirt. "Dewey?" She pointed over his shoulder.

"What's wrong?" He turned. "Motherfucker." He blinked, staring at Big Cal holding a machine gun.

Next to him, Hillary glided across the pavement with her hands firmly planted on her hips and a smug grin on her face.

Dewey: Big Cal is HERE.

Dewey turned and came face to face with the enemy. "What the hell are you doing, Hillary?" Dewey put a protective arm around Magnolia.

Magnolia trembled, tucking her body behind his, holding on to his waist.

"That man is bad news." Dewey puffed out his chest, scanning the area, but everyone had left. They couldn't be too far away. Hank would send help, and soon.

Hillary tilted her head. "Please don't speak badly about my boyfriend."

"Jesus, Hillary. It was you who fucked with my plane, wasn't it?" Dewey's lungs burned. "Why? You could have killed us."

"That was the point," Big Cal said. "I underestimated my own flesh and blood. I didn't think she'd go to her mother, who decided to cut a deal with Feds and now my business partners are worried."

"Killing Magnolia isn't going to change whatever can of worms Flower opened up," Dewey said.

"No. It won't. But by morning Flower will be dead," Big Cal said.

Out of the corner of Dewey's eye, he saw movement on the roof of the hangar. Dakota made himself known for a brief second. Dewey's pulse increased.

"And what do you plan on doing with me?" Dewey knew the answer, but he needed to keep him talking while his team set up and did a full sweep. Who knew how many of Big Cal's crew were lurking in the bushes. The private jet that Hillary worked for had the capacity for eight passengers. That meant there could be at least seven heavily armed men on the property, somewhere.

Or still in the plane.

Watching.

That might not be good.

"That's a dumb question for such a smart guy," Big Cal said. "You should be asking how I'm going to kill you, because I can't just shoot you up and think no one will come looking for me."

"Everyone will know it was you," Magnolia said. "Between the tattoo and the connections to my mother, it will be impossible for you to get away with it."

"What tattoo?" He lifted his shirt over his shoulder. "You see, I turned over a new leaf years ago. I had it removed because I didn't want to be reminded of my sordid past. And your mother and her constituents were trying to set me up."

"That's a pretty tall tale," Dewey said.

"I've been planning it for two years, and a few months ago, when I met Hillary, it all fell into place." He looped his arm around her shoulders.

She smiled as if she won the lottery.

Dewey's stomach churned. "All right. I'll bite. How are you going to kill us?"

"I'm not. Hillary's going to. Love triangles and crazy women." He grabbed the back of Hillary's hair and yanked it. Hard.

"Ouch. You're hurting me." Hillary reached up behind her and grabbed Big Cal's wrists.

"Oh, shut the fuck up, bitch," Big Cal said.

"You're a fucking piece of work." Dewey lunged forward.

Big Cal raised his weapon, slamming it into Hillary's gut. She fell to her knees, scraping them on the pavement.

Magnolia gripped Dewey's forearm.

"Cal, what are you doing?" Hillary looked up at Big Cal with tears in her eyes.

He pulled her to her feet.

She stumbled in her high heels.

Holding her tight, he pulled out a handgun and put it in Hillary's hand, raising her arm. She shook her head, refusing to close her fingers around the handle.

Well, fuck. Dewey reached out and tucked Magnolia behind him.

"Let her go," Big Cal said.

"Excuse me?" Dewey sucked in a deep breath. He had a good idea how this was going to play out. He took a quick glance toward the hangar. If anyone had a good shot, they would have taken it.

"Actually." Big Cal untucked his shirt, showing a holster. He kicked a second smaller weapon toward Dewey. "Put this in her hand."

"You want me to shoot your girlfriend?" Magnolia asked.

"Now you're talking like my daughter," Big Cal said.

"Cal. This isn't funny." Hillary tried to take a step back. "Why are you doing this?"

"Take the fucking gun, Hillary." He turned the harness on the machine gun so it hung on his back. "You had no problem killing them a few hours ago." He stood behind Hillary, who flapped her hands, trying not to touch the small weapon.

"But now you're talking about killing me too," Hillary pleaded.

"A small price to pay for my freedom," Big Cal said.

Magnolia bent over and picked up the weapon. She held it in her hands as if she knew how to use it.

Dewey had seen her more than once with her own handgun, he just wasn't sure how well she could handle it.

"Stop fighting me, Hillary." Big Cal took the butt of the pistol and smacked her across the face with it.

"So, who kills Dewey?" Magnolia asked with a calm voice.

"I don't give a shit. I'll kill you all. I just need your

prints on the weapons," Big Cal said. "And you played right into it." He laughed.

"No. You're the one who just got played." Magnolia raised the gun. "The apple doesn't fall far from the tree, Dad."

Before Dewey could blink, Magnolia raised her arms. "Hit the ground, Hillary."

"What the fuck?" Big Cal just stood there.

Hillary dropped to her hands and knees.

Pop! Pop! Pop!

The first shot hit Big Cal's hand, and he jerked back. The second one landed on his shoulder. The third one nailed him in his knee cap.

"You fucking little bitch." He tumbled to the ground, fumbling for the machine gun.

Pop!

She fired again, hitting his other knee. "The only good thing my mother taught me was how to shoot a gun. I'm an excellent marksman."

Dewey raced toward Big Cal, snatching up both the machine gun and the small weapon. The sound of boots clamoring on the pavement caught his attention. He glanced in the direction of the hangar. Maddog, Clayton, and Dakota appeared from their hiding places.

Sirens rang out in the background.

He turned his attention to Magnolia. "Um. Babe. You can put that thing down now."

"Oh. Sorry." She set it on the ground and rubbed her hands on her legs.

"Hillary, are you okay?" He helped her to her feet.

"No. No, I'm not." She covered her face and cried.

He patted her back, pawning her off on Maddog, who didn't look very happy about the prospect.

Dewey quickly closed the gap, taking her into his arms. "You never told me you knew how to handle a gun."

"I honestly hate them. My mom and dad used to make me go target shooting, and it sucked that I was so good at it."

"It's a good skill, especially when you know how to maim, not kill." He kissed her forehead.

"I don't think I could live with myself if I took a human life. Even one as horrible as…as…as…I can't believe he's my father."

"Sperm doesn't make someone a parent."

"What if my children turn out like my parents?"

"You didn't turn out like them, so why would your kids?" He cupped her face. "You're the best person I know. I love you, Magnolia."

"I love you, too." She dropped her head to his chest. "When will your plane be fixed?"

"It will be a while. Why?"

"I want to fly again."

"I have access to other planes. I can make that happen anytime you want," he said. "But first I'd like to take a week or two and do nothing but feed you breakfast in bed."

"I'm not going to say no to that," she said. "But I think it's safe to say I won't be needing that new identity."

EPILOGUE

THREE MONTHS LATER...

MAGNOLIA LAY on the hospital bed holding Dewey's hand. "I'm fine. Really. You are seriously overreacting."

"That's the second time you passed out this week. Not to mention you've lost weight and you have no appetite. Something's not right."

"First off." She waved her finger under Dewey's nose. "To say I fainted is being dramatic. I've got a bug that is lingering. It's no big deal. Relax."

"I want a doctor to tell me that." One thing she'd learned about Dewey is that not only could he be a little protective, but he was also stubborn and pigheaded. Qualities she found endearing, except for in this particular moment.

"It's a little ridiculous to whisk me off to the emergency room." Of course, she was the one who got in the car with little protest. She had to admit, if only to herself, the dizzy spells did frighten her since she'd had more than she'd told Dewey about.

Not to mention, she struggled to keep down food on a regular basis.

The curtain swished open, and Doctor Murphy entered the exam room. "Sorry I had to step out for a moment."

"Not a problem." Magnolia fiddled with the sheet. She'd never been a fan of doctors or hospitals.

"So, how long have you been feeling under the weather?" the doctor asked.

"A couple of weeks," she said. "Maybe three. It comes in waves. And I generally start the day out feeling pretty good. However, as the hours tick on, my stomach starts to churn, and I just feel off."

"And she's getting worse," Dewey added. "She doesn't eat hardly anything."

"Have you been vomiting? Diarrhea? That kind of thing?" The doctor listened to her lungs and heart while he rubbed her neck, checking out her tonsils.

"Just the throwing up. It's not all the time and it happens randomly," she said.

"Can you lay down for me?" the doctor asked.

Dewey got all weird and jumped off the side of the bed, helping her to her back. "She gets really tired in the afternoon, which is when her stomach is usually at its worst. But it's the mornings when these dizzy spells hit her the hardest."

"Have you ever gotten migraines before?" the

doctor asked as he pushed on her belly.

"No. And I'm not getting headaches."

"Huh." The doctor glanced to the ceiling. "When was your last period?"

"I generally don't get them with the pill I'm on. I mean sometimes I get a really light one," she said.

"Okay. When was your last really light one?" The doctor pressed with both hands.

"A few months ago, I guess," she said, letting out a long breath as she glanced at Dewey.

"Doc. What's wrong?" Dewey asked.

"I don't know that anything's wrong." The doctor tucked his hands in his lab coat. "But I'd like to do an ultrasound."

"Why?" Magnolia asked.

"Your uterus is swollen."

"What does that mean? Does she have a tumor or something?" Dewey took her hand and squeezed it hard.

"Is your boyfriend always this doom and gloom?"

"No. This is a side of him I haven't seen yet." She shifted, making a little more room for Dewey to sit. "But I have to say, while I'm not quite as freaked out as he is, I'm concerned about everything you're saying."

"I could rattle off a few of the things that I think could be going on, most are not serious at all, but I won't know anything until I get that ultrasound. It won't take long at all. I'll be back shortly."

The doctor disappeared into the hallway.

Magnolia had to admit, she was spooked. But she couldn't let Dewey know how much. The man was losing his shit. "Come on, you big oaf." She scooted over, pressing her back up to the side railing, making even more room. "Come give me a hug."

"I should have made you come in sooner." Dewey wrapped his arms around her, kissing her temple.

"I'm sure it's nothing major." She rested her head on his chest and closed her eyes. "Did you see the flowers we got from my mother?"

"She seems to be doing well in her halfway house," Dewey said. "Staying mostly out of trouble."

"I still don't really want her in my life. I can't forgive her for all the things she's done to me, but I don't hate her."

"You know I'll support you with whatever you want."

"I know." How she'd gotten so lucky with Dewey, she'd never know. And she didn't want to question it. She'd found home, and she wasn't ever going to leave.

Doctor Murphy returned with a young woman pushing a piece of equipment.

"This is Katie," the doctor said. "She's going to do the ultrasound, but she can't do it with him on the bed."

"You're killing me, Doc," Dewey said.

"We're going to be doing this the uncomfortable

way." Katie held up a large wand. She covered it with what could only be described as a condom. "This isn't any different from a pelvic exam."

"Okeydokey." Magnolia reached out for Dewey's hand. She held his gaze.

He mouthed *I love you.*

She did her best not to grimace as they started the procedure. It truly wasn't all that terrible, just awkward.

And a tad frightening as the longer the doctor and Katie stared at the little monitor and remained quiet, only glancing occasionally at each other while the doctor pointed, and Katie tapped on a keyboard with her free hand.

"As I suspected," the doctor said.

"What's wrong with her?" Dewey asked.

"I wouldn't describe this particular situation using that word." The doctor turned the monitor and tapped the screen. "We're going to need to figure out why your birth control failed because you're about eight weeks pregnant—with twins."

Magnolia rubbed her eyes and leaned forward. "Are you kidding me?"

"There is baby number one." The doctor made a circle with his finger. "And that is baby number two."

"Holy shit," Magnolia mumbled.

"I think I need to sit down," Dewey said.

"Wait. Dewey." Magnolia held up her hand. "There's no chair—"

Crash!

"Shit. That hurt." Dewey waved arm as he lay on the tiled floor.

"Are you okay?" Katie asked.

"No. Yes. I don't know." Dewey managed to stand up and make it back to Magnolia's bedside. "Don't women get morning sickness when this happens?"

"Some do. Others get all day sickness," the doctor said. "We're still waiting on all your blood work, so it's going to be a while before I can discharge you. I'll send down someone from the OB/GYN department to talk to you. Since this is such a shock, and a multiple birth, they can guide you through what to expect."

"Thanks, Doc, we appreciate it," Dewey said.

Magnolia had turned her attention back to the screen and the image of two babies with two little heartbeats.

She reached out and traced the little gray blobs with her fingers.

Those were her children. She and Dewey would be charged with making sure they were fed and bathed and give them the things they needed to survive. More importantly, they were responsible for loving them.

But she already did.

She never thought she could love anyone as much as she'd loved Dewey. They'd only been together for about four months. They'd just moved in together a few weeks ago. They'd tossed around the idea of getting married, but that was maybe a few months down the road.

And kids? Well, that was still one of those topics that they weren't quite on the same page about. It wasn't that she didn't want them; she just wasn't sure she wanted to birth them.

Tears burned in her eyes.

Never in her life did she want anything so much as she wanted those two little babies. She pressed her hand against her stomach.

"Hey." Dewey kissed her temple. "I hadn't even thought about this as a possible outcome."

"Neither had I." She glanced around the room, unaware that Katie and the doctor had left. "This is a lot to take in," Magnolia said.

Dewey sat on the edge of the bed. He took her chin with his thumb and his forefinger. "Your eyes are sparkling like I've never seen before."

"I never thought I could be this happy." She palmed his cheek. "It's like flying. I was so afraid of the unknown, and then the first time we crash-landed." She laughed, shaking her head. "And you had to knock me up, while I'm on the pill, with twins no less. Who does that?"

"I do." He patted her nose. "Dakota and Alabama are going to be so jealous. They were disappointed when they found out they weren't having twins."

"Nah. They'll just have another kid." She waved

her hand.

"So, how about we take that trip to Vegas?" he said with a bright smile. "It seems like a good weekend to get married."

"I think that's the best idea you've had in a long time." She leaned in and kissed him, hard and with intent.

This was the family she was destined to belong with. This was the family she chose.

Magnolia had found home.

Thank you for taking the time to read SAVING MAGNLIA. Please feel free to leave an honest review on Amazon!

Sign up for my Newsletter (https://dl.bookfunnel.com/6atcf7g1be) where I often give away free books before publication.

JOIN my private Facebook group (https://www.facebook.com/groups/191706547909047/) where I post exclusive excerpts and discuss all things murder and love!

Never miss a new release. Follow me on Amazon:amazon.com/author/jentalty
And on Bookbub: bookbub.com/authors/jen-talty

THE LAST FLIGHT

THE RETURN HOME

THE MATRIARCH

The Collective Order

THE LOST SISTER

THE LOST SOLDIER

THE LOST SOUL

THE LOST CONNECTION

A Spin-Off Series: Witches Academy Series

THE NEW ORDER

Special Forces Operation Alpha

BURNING DESIRE

BURNING KISS

BURNING SKIES

BURNING LIES

BURNING HEART

BURNING BED

REMEMBER ME ALWAYS

The Brotherhood Protectors

Out of the Wild

ROUGH JUSTICE

ROUGH AROUND THE EDGES

ROUGH RIDE

ROUGH EDGE

ROUGH BEAUTY

The Brotherhood Protectors

The Saving Series

SAVING LOVE

SAVING MAGNOLIA

Holiday Romances

A CHRISTMAS GETAWAY

ALASKAN CHRISTMAS

WHISPERS

Heroes & Heroines on the Field

TAKING A RISK

TEE TIME

The Twilight Crossing Series

THE BLIND DATE

SPRING FLING

SUMMER'S GONE

WINTER WEDDING

Witches and Werewolves

LADY SASS

ALL THAT SASS

ABOUT JEN TALTY

Welcome to my World! I'm a USA Today Bestseller of Romantic Suspense, Contemporary Romance, and Paranormal Romance.

I first started writing while carting my kids to one hockey rink after the other, averaging 170 games per year between 3 kids in 2 countries and 5 states. My first book, IN TWO WEEKS was originally published in 2007. In 2010 I helped form a publishing company (Cool Gus Publishing) with NY Times Bestselling Author Bob Mayer where I ran the technical side of the business through 2016.

I'm currently enjoying the next phase of my life...the empty NESTER! My husband and I spend our winters in Jupiter, Florida and our summers in Rochester, NY. We have three amazing children who have all gone off to carve out their places in the world, while I continue to craft stories that I hope will make you readers feel good and put a smile on your face.

Sign up for my Newsletter (https://dl.bookfunnel.com/

6atcf7g1be) where I often give away free books before publication.

Join my private Facebook group (https://www.facebook. com/groups/191706547909047/) where I post exclusive excerpts and discuss all things murder and love!

Never miss a new release. Follow me on Amazon:
amazon.com/author/jentalty
And on Bookbub:
bookbub.com/authors/jen-talty

BROTHERHOOD PROTECTORS

ORIGINAL SERIES BY ELLE JAMES

Brotherhood Protectors Series

Montana SEAL (#1)

Bride Protector SEAL (#2)

Montana D-Force (#3)

Cowboy D-Force (#4)

Montana Ranger (#5)

Montana Dog Soldier (#6)

Montana SEAL Daddy (#7)

Montana Ranger's Wedding Vow (#8)

Montana SEAL Undercover Daddy (#9)

Cape Cod SEAL Rescue (#10)

Montana SEAL Friendly Fire (#11)

Montana SEAL's Mail-Order Bride (#12)

SEAL Justice (#13)

Ranger Creed (#14)

Delta Force Rescue (#15)

Montana Rescue (Sleeper SEAL)

Hot SEAL Salty Dog (SEALs in Paradise)

Hot SEAL Hawaiian Nights (SEALs in Paradise)

ABOUT ELLE JAMES

ELLE JAMES also writing as MYLA JACKSON is a *New York Times* and *USA Today* Bestselling author of books including cowboys, intrigues and paranormal adventures that keep her readers on the edges of their seats. With over eighty works in a variety of sub-genres and lengths she has published with Harlequin, Samhain, Ellora's Cave, Kensington, Cleis Press, and Avon. When she's not at her computer, she's traveling, snow skiing, boating, or riding her ATV, dreaming up new stories. Learn more about Elle James at www.ellejames.com

Website | Facebook | Twitter | GoodReads | Newsletter | BookBub | Amazon

Follow Elle!
www.ellejames.com
ellejames@ellejames.com

facebook.com/ellejamesauthor
twitter.com/ElleJamesAuthor